# Broken Promises

ANITA PEREZ FERGUSON

BROKEN PROMISES
by Anita Perez Ferguson

Published by:
Luz Publications P.O. Box 90651 Santa Barbara CA 93190

Copyright © 2023 Anita Perez Ferguson

ISBN 978-0-9673300-8-2 (paperback)
ISBN 978-0-9673300-3-7 (eBook)

All rights reserved. No part of this publication may be reproduced, stored in a retrieval system, or transmitted in any form or by any means, electronic, mechanical, photocopying, recording or otherwise, without the prior written permission of the publisher.

Publisher's Cataloging-In-Publication Data
(Prepared by The Donohue Group, Inc.)

Names: Perez Ferguson, Anita, author.
Title: Broken Promises / Anita Perez Ferguson.
Description: Santa Barbara, CA: Luz Publications, [2023] | Series: [Mission bells]; [book 3] | Interest age level: 014-020. | Summary "Sparrow, a half-Chumash Indigenous girl, eavesdrops on her father's conversation and overhears his plan to forcibly remove the governor of Alta California and acquire the Mexican territory for the US. Her tribal family and Native customs are threatened. Sparrow must decide whether to keep her father's secret but lose her homeland or warn her mother and the Mexican authorities but lose her father's love." — Provided by publisher.

Identifiers: ISBN 978-0-9673300-8-2 Subjects: LCSH: History—19th century—Fiction. | California——History—19th century—Fiction. | Forced labor—California—History—19th century—Fiction. | Hispanic Americans—History—18th century—Fiction. | Missions, Spanish— California—Indigenous persons—History—19th century—Fiction. | Young adult fiction.

Classification: LCC PS3616.E743 T95 2020 | DDC 813/.6 [Fic]—dc23

Disclaimer: This is a work of fiction. All characters, names, incidents and dialogue in this novel are either the products of the author's imagination or are used fictitiously. Any resemblance to actual events, locations or persons, living or dead, is entirely coincidental.

Printed in the United States of America

# Acknowledging Those Who Came Before Us

**It is my pleasure to** thank all the professionals and friends who helped to bring this book to fruition. There have been many who supported the writing and production of *Broken Promises*. Thanks go to my husband, Bill, my sisters, my many friends, and the other authors who cheered me on. The professionals at Bublish have made my books possible. I thank Adrienne Abate Kaplan, illustrator, for our *Broken Promises* Family Tree. I also thank my nephew, Paul Sweeney, and my cousin, David Gillespie, for encouraging me by keeping our own family tree of ancestors current.

The careful edit by Stacey Parshall Jensen, sensitivity reader, diversity editor, and cultural consultant, was a great help to my respectful representation of Sparrow, the bicultural teen heroine, and her cultural heritage. Joining my friends at We Need Diverse Books (WNDB diversebooks.org), I believe that a variety of voices must come forward to educate and encourage our current student population. Some of those voices emerge from within us, from our ancestors and our spiritual traditions. My own inspirations are planted in the common history of many

Latin American persons who share a mixed heritage. Mixtecs are indigenous Mesoamerican peoples of a particular region of Mexico. After Cortez landed in 1519, European (Spanish) blood began to mingle with Indigenous persons. New peoples, experiences, and stories emerged—our stories.

With respect to my paternal great-great-great-grandfather:

Antonio Lopez, born 1795 in Zacatlàn, Puebla, Mexico.

Also to my maternal great-great-grandmother:

Maria Ignacia Gutierrez, born 1835 in Cusihuiriachi, Chihuahua, Mexico.

# Acknowledging Those Who Came Before Us

**It is my pleasure to** thank all the professionals and friends who helped to bring this book to fruition. There have been many who supported the writing and production of *Broken Promises*. Thanks go to my husband, Bill, my sisters, my many friends, and the other authors who cheered me on. The professionals at Bublish have made my books possible. I thank Adrienne Abate Kaplan, illustrator, for our *Broken Promises* Family Tree. I also thank my nephew, Paul Sweeney, and my cousin, David Gillespie, for encouraging me by keeping our own family tree of ancestors current.

The careful edit by Stacey Parshall Jensen, sensitivity reader, diversity editor, and cultural consultant, was a great help to my respectful representation of Sparrow, the bicultural teen heroine, and her cultural heritage. Joining my friends at We Need Diverse Books (WNDB diversebooks.org), I believe that a variety of voices must come forward to educate and encourage our current student population. Some of those voices emerge from within us, from our ancestors and our spiritual traditions. My own inspirations are planted in the common history of many

Latin American persons who share a mixed heritage. Mixtecs are indigenous Mesoamerican peoples of a particular region of Mexico. After Cortez landed in 1519, European (Spanish) blood began to mingle with Indigenous persons. New peoples, experiences, and stories emerged—our stories.

With respect to my paternal great-great-great-grandfather:

Antonio Lopez, born 1795 in Zacatlàn, Puebla, Mexico.

Also to my maternal great-great-grandmother:

Maria Ignacia Gutierrez, born 1835 in Cusihuiriachi, Chihuahua, Mexico.

*Heteromelus arbutifolia*
Qwé berry or toyon

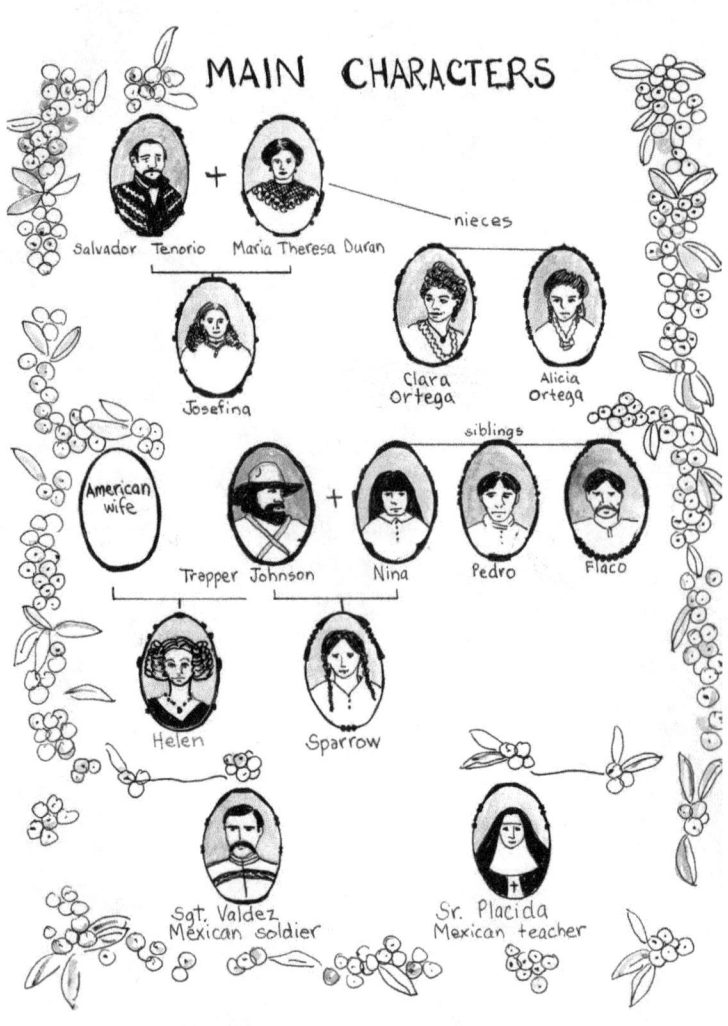

Adrienne Abate Kaplan, Illustrator

# 01
## Chapter

"**Not too many of those** red berries. They will make you sleep forever," Sparrow's mother told her as they collected herbs on a hilltop overlooking the Pacific. "Your grandma called this toyon. People here call them *Qwé* berries."

Sparrow cared little about picking berries today. She was disturbed to see how enormous her hands looked. When would her body stop growing? Would any boy ever choose to hold her gigantic hands?

"Use three berries for a grieving woman." Mama Nina passed on the family's healing customs. "Never five, or you rest with the ancestors."

"You mean that?" Sparrow pulled back from the bush. "But why would anybody eat so many?"

"In this life, many suffer—defeated warriors, heartbroken widows, and desperate souls. You will understand." The herbs grew in the shade, overlooking the harbor in Monterey, Alta California. Brown pelicans flew in formation on the ocean breezes. "See the birds? They release seeds to grow new plants here. We all have a purpose."

"When will I learn all these things? What is my special purpose?" Sparrow moved clumsily, unaccustomed to the changes taking place in her body. In some ways, she resembled Mama Nina's people, the Chumash, with her dark hair and eyes. "Why do I grow so tall?" Her long legs, enormous feet, and large hands were like Papa's, who was an American.

"You will know your purpose when it is your time. It is our way." Mama Nina bent to gather handfuls of coyote brush. "See this? It is good for skin burns and rash. We also use it for tea." She pushed the brush into her sack. "You grow tall like your papa, Sparrow, not like my people. This is as it should be."

"I may be half-good—the part of me with your Indian blood. But these enormous feet do not fit into my shoes. When Papa comes back, I need new shoes to impress him." Sparrow's slippers were made from her friend Josefina's castoffs.

"You need new shoes for new journeys." Mama Nina looked down at Sparrow's feet. "I see you are outgrowing those hand-me-downs."

"He is coming back, right?" Sparrow's papa never visited now that his American family had moved to Monterey. Still, Sparrow knew she would see her papa again, even though the newcomers were disturbing Native ways and tribal people were disappearing from the territory.

Mama Nina moved toward the pathway that wound down the hill, back to Rancho Duran. It was scattered with wildflowers.

"Look at the poppies, so bright!" Sparrow imagined the flowers in a colorful bouquet. Would Sparrow ever have a beau who plucked blooms for her?

"Poppies are bad medicine. Many beautiful flowers fade away, Sparrow." Mama Nina was practical. The healing blossoms

# Broken Promises

she carried—Qwè berries, coyote brush, sage, and mint—were not so colorful. After Papa abandoned them, Mama had started caring for patients using these herbs, so she could in turn take care of Sparrow.

# Broken Promises

she carried—Qwè berries, coyote brush, sage, and mint—were not so colorful. After Papa abandoned them, Mama had started caring for patients using these herbs, so she could in turn take care of Sparrow.

# 02

## Chapter

**Every morning, at sunrise, Sparrow** followed Mama Nina to the hilltop to collect herbs and berries or down to the creek to collect water and the small fish caught in their submerged basket traps. Then there were other land traps to check for small animals that they skinned and dried for jerky. Mama's people lived off the land, and now she taught Sparrow all their skills and traditions.

"Here, for our tea." Sparrow collected pieces of honeycomb from a nearby beehive. She loved sweets, and not everything Sparrow ate came from the natural world around her. This was a secret that separated Sparrow from her mama.

The two of them lived in a one-room wooden cabin that also served as Mama Nina's herbal clinic. The space was so small that Mama had to roll their sleeping blankets into the corner each morning to make room for her clients.

"Find high, dry spaces between the wooden planks to protect the herbs from the damp air and the mice," Sparrow's mother told her. They each had their morning chores, and then Sparrow and her mother shared hot tea, berries, and little dry cakes made from ground acorns for their morning meal. The cabin could have been cozy, but it was originally a storage shed used to butcher and store prey, so the space smelled of dead deer, bears, and wolves.

"We need more sage bundles to clear the air." The odor of death lingered no matter how many times Mama Nina spread the vapors.

Their cabin was on the property of Señor Salvador Tenorio, whose wife, Señora Maria Theresa Duran Tenorio, received regular herbal treatments from Mama Nina. Señora Tenorio allowed Mama Nina and Sparrow to live in the cabin in exchange for her treatments. Sparrow often daydreamed about living in the Tenorios' big hacienda.

"They have a perfect life in that big house. I wish we were like them." Sparrow attended school with the Tenorios' daughter, Josefina. Just beyond their small cabin, red clay tiles lead to the hacienda courtyard. The house was built in the shape of a square, with a patio in the middle where flowers grew and little baskets with singing yellow birds hung from overhead beams. Sparrow often saw Josefina's aunt Alicia and her sweetheart, Sergeant Valdez, meeting there, and she often imagined the lovebirds' conversations in the shadows.

"Just remember, many beautiful things are fragile," Mama Nina said, waving one more bundle of sage leaves to cleanse the cabin air.

Josefina's parents hosted parties for community leaders in their huge hacienda. Guests included visiting captains, artists, and musicians. Josefina's aunt Clara, who also lived in the hacienda, conducted all the family's social arrangements. She knew everyone in town and all about the latest fashions. Sparrow often served refreshments for the guests at these parties. It was on these occasions that Josefina sneaked Sparrow sweet treats from the hacienda's kitchen. Sparrow's mouth watered just to think of sampling the refreshments. The girls sometimes eavesdropped on the partygoers' conversations.

Lately, all the conversations were about the Americans trying to take territory away from Mexico and take power from Governor Alvarado. They wanted the land from San Diego in the south all the way past Fort Ross in the north, where the Russians had already taken land from the Native people. The United States envoys tempted public officials with special benefits described in a proposed treaty named after Guadalupe Hidalgo. If an agreement was not made by 1845, the only alternative was war with the Americans. No one wanted that. With only one year left to decide, the treaty was a subject Sparrow and Josefina studied at the convent school they attended.

"I'll be late for class if I don't leave for school now." Sparrow told a little lie to Mama. She put on the shoes that pinched her feet and hurried off. But she did not go directly to school. Instead, she detoured to the Monterey harbor. Ever since Papa had left to live with his American family, the only place Sparrow was sure to see him was at the docks where he worked. She'd found a perfect hiding place to watch him, but she never let him see her, and they never spoke. Just being near him as he tended to the cargo ships made her feel they still experienced something together.

# 03

## Chapter

**When Sparrow arrived at the** harbor in the early morning hours, the waters in Mexico's Monterey Bay were like glass. The mirrored surface reflected the long-necked shore birds. Seagulls roosted on the sailing masts and squawked their demands for fish entrails and other scraps of food.

Larger ships, two and three tiers high, were anchored out in the bay. Each ship flew a colorful flag. Sparrow studied the home-port colors of the foreign ships from France, England, and Spain and those of the American ships. Some of their vessels were fitted with portholes for cannons, but these warships were only used for peacetime trade in this Mexican port.

As Sparrow grew, it had become more difficult to hide herself between the shipping crates. Her hips grazed the packing ropes, and her shoulders were wedged between the boxes. She stayed still and listened for her papa's voice. He worked with other foreign sailors, checking cargo, counting hides, and swapping the news from various ports. Papa knew many of the men from his days working with the American Scientific Expedition. He'd been working for them as a surveyor when he first met Sparrow's mama and became impressed with her knowledge of the lands, rivers, and plants in the Mexican territory. That had been seventeen years ago.

Today, his conversation with the other sailors went on and on. The men's voices were easy to hear because they spoke loudly, bragged often, and boasted about their trapping skills or something they were planning with Papa.

"If your men are prepared, I will show you his routines. Leave it to me." The fellow who spoke had curly black hair and bushy eyebrows, and his voice thundered. He wore some kind of uniform jacket—not Mexican—with a red, white, and blue striped armband.

Papa looked around the dock, but Sparrow remained hidden behind the crates. "If we work together, the governor will soon be out of our way." Then he continued, "Our troops are ready. War is certain, and when we are victorious, this dock will fly the American flag."

Two other sailors with ruddy faces and red beards shook their fists in the air. Their shabby uniforms were a faded blue and yellow.

Sparrow tried to make sense of their conversation. What were they planning? Governor Alvarado was a friend of the Tenorio family. He had attended many of their parties. Sparrow's hands felt wet and cold.

*Out of the way?* Those were the words Papa had used. He sounded like he was going to become a traitor. Sparrow squirmed to stay between the packing crates, pressing her lips together to keep herself from calling out, "You can't do that!" Her knees were pressed together, too. She was nervous and needed to relieve herself soon.

## BROKEN PROMISES

Then another man approached—Josefina's father, Salvador Tenorio, who served as the Mexican harbormaster in Monterey.

"Let's keep business moving, men." Salvador Tenorio spoke with an air of authority and interrupted Papa's conversation with the plotting sailors. "Is everything all right here?" Salvador and Papa had known each other long ago, when they were young men. The two men only saw each other on the dock now that Papa had abandoned Mama and Sparrow and Señora Tenorio had forbidden Papa from coming to the hacienda.

"Yes, sir, good cargo. I've collected the dock fees. You can be on your way now, sailors," Papa said, sending the other men away as if nothing was amiss.

"Stop them. Tell him," Sparrow muttered to herself. How could her papa be making such plans with these men? Was Papa really a spy for the Americans?

When the coast was clear, Sparrow wriggled her body out of her hiding spot, intending to make her way to the convent school. She wrestled with what she'd heard Papa say. If she told Mama, she would have to admit she'd been spying on Papa at the dock. She couldn't tell Josefina, her best friend, because then all the girls at school would soon know. If she reported what she'd overheard to anybody, Papa and his friends would be jailed, maybe even exiled from Alta California. She could never reveal Papa's secret.

# 04

## Chapter

**Sparrow carried the burden of** her papa's secret plan with her to the convent school, where the morning classes were almost over. The school building had once served as the pueblo's only chapel, and the old school bell had once been used to call the people to Mass. Today, the bell simply clanged for the students' lunch break. The old wooden pews were reused as benches for students. The priest's pulpit was where the head teacher at the convent school, Sister Placida, stood to make special announcements to the students, who were all teenage girls from wealthy Mexican families—all except for Sparrow.

Sparrow entered through the back door of the classroom long after the day's lectures had begun. From her vantage point, she could identify the girls by the dark braids hanging down their backs. One new student was an American named Helen, who had curly yellow hair. Sparrow looked at her with great suspicion. This girl had enrolled at the school after Papa moved away from Mama Nina and Sparrow.

"You're late again. Where were you?" Josefina asked, leaning toward Sparrow. "Sister Placida was asking for you this morning." Her book was open, and she kept a ruler under each line to follow what the teachers said. "You caused me to lose my place."

"I met my papa at the dock." Sparrow told a little lie, loud enough for the yellow-haired girl, Helen, to hear her. "We are making big plans together." She wished it were true. If only she had not heard Papa's real intentions. She prayed the new girl was not who she thought.

"Tell me more at lunchtime," Josefina said as she moved her ruler down the page. "I mean, tell me everything." The two girls rarely had any secrets between them. Sparrow squirmed in her seat. Students could not relax on the floor, legs crossed, the way she preferred to sit.

The other girls at school were unfriendly toward Sparrow, and none of them were Native girls. They were the daughters of prosperous Mexican ranchers and dressed in starched pinafores. Sparrow was taller than all of them, and she wore the apron she'd used for collecting herbs with Mama earlier that morning. She slumped down in her seat and picked at bits of fern and willow fuzz stuck to her hem, hoping to be ignored.

The hour before lunchtime dragged on with the recitation of their new vocabulary words: forthright, scrupulous, reliable, stalwart, loyal. Sparrow clenched her jaw as every new word stabbed at her conscience. Should she keep Papa's secret? Or should she share his plan with someone and ask for help? If she told, would Papa ever forgive her?

Minutes before the lunch bell rang, Sister Placida walked straight toward Sparrow. She wore her black habit and white bib, on top of which lay a large brass cross. The nun paused, clutching her Bible and her red writing book.

"Young lady, you will meet with the teachers during the noon meal." Sister Placida forced a smile and lowered her voice, but all the girls turned around to see who she spoke to. Helen glared at Sparrow from her seat in the front row.

Sparrow's heart raced, and her words stuck in her throat. All she could do was nod and follow the sister to lunch. How could news of Papa's treachery have spread so fast? No matter what the nuns did to her, she would not give up his plans.

## Chapter 05

**Sparrow held her breath as** she entered the nuns' dining room. She kept her head low and caught sight of her dirty apron and ill-fitting shoes. She was relieved when Sister Placida paused to speak with Josefina's aunt Alicia, who taught at the school but was not a part of the holy order of nuns. "Miss Alicia, your lesson about our local flowers and herbs received high praise from everyone. Congratulations."

Sparrow had helped Aunt Alicia teach the lesson on plants and herbs, and it had made the other schoolgirls jealous.

"Thank you, Sister. I had an excellent helper." Aunt Alicia turned to Sparrow and winked. Sparrow blushed. "She could be an excellent teacher someday." Alicia's words surprised Sparrow, and her eyes darted between the two women.

Then Sister Placida pointed at a chair with her chin, instructing Sparrow to sit.

"I don't feel very well," Sparrow said, needing to make some excuse to leave the room. If Aunt Alicia heard from Sister

Placida about Papa's treachery, everyone at the hacienda would know—including Mama.

"Here, take some soup and bread. You'll feel better." Aunt Alicia was always so kind. Sparrow did feel better when she took a bite of bread spread thick with fresh butter, but her stomach was still in knots. When would the nun break the bad news about Papa?

"We are inviting younger novices into our teaching order," Sister Placida said, glancing around the dining room at the aging nuns. "Please mention the idea to Sparrow's mother. Perhaps Señora Tenorio could sponsor Sparrow as a teacher, too."

"I will do just that." Aunt Alicia's voice sounded a bit stern to Sparrow. She had not known Señora Tenorio was her sponsor. Would she consider sponsoring Sparrow to teach if she learned Papa was plotting to be a conspirator? "So, Sparrow, how do you respond to the invitation to join the nuns?" Aunt Alicia asked.

Sparrow opened her mouth, but no sound came out.

"A girl her age never knows her mind, much less God's divine purpose for her life," Sister Placida interjected. "I was confused when I was rescued from my poor home and blessed to become a novice. But I gained a calling and a family. That is what I believe our Lord wants for Sparrow."

"I have a home, and a mama," Sparrow muttered. "She needs me."

"Come, come, my dear. It is Señora Tenorio who provides your room. Your mama has work to do, and you are often late to class. You could be a bright student if you applied yourself." Sister Placida glanced down at Sparrow's feet. "We are offering you a future of important work and service, a room, meals, clothing. . . and shoes."

"It's a lovely opportunity. I will speak to your mama, Sparrow, as the sister asks." Aunt Alicia wrapped her arm around Sparrow's slumped shoulders. "We should leave now. We have news to share."

## Broken Promises

Sparrow felt safe with Aunt Alicia's arm around her shoulders. She was so relieved Papa's secret was still protected that she took a deep breath when they left the dining room. Now she had this unexpected invitation from Sister Placida to share. She stood straight, and her lips formed a little smile. She knew the other students would watch them leave the schoolyard with expressions of curiosity and coldness. They would assume she was in trouble and had been dismissed from school for tardiness. Everyone stared at Sparrow wearing Josefina's old dress under her apron, the seams strained by her growing figure.

# 06

## Chapter

**When they reached the hacienda**, Aunt Alicia's sister, Clara, was the only one at home. She stood in the sala, wearing flimsy under garments, a pink camisole, and a ruffled slip. Next to her was a gigantic suitcase overflowing with colorful frocks, shawls, and party garments.

"I just can't decide what to wear. I'm so glad you are here to help." Clara pulled garments out of the trunk, held them up, and then tossed them aside, one after another.

"I'm not helpful in judging clothes." Aunt Alicia put her books and satchel down on a table, beckoning Sparrow into the house from where she remained near the patio door. "Don't be shy. It's just us women."

"Who are you talking to?" Clara turned to see Sparrow in the doorway. "Oh, it's you. Why aren't you in school?" She didn't wait for an answer. "No matter, I need to tell you about our party this Saturday. You will serve many important people. I hope you will not be wearing that old apron." After looking

Sparrow up and down, Clara continued tossing dresses around like rags.

Sparrow was embarrassed to look at Clara as she noticed Clara's full bust. Was that what she should expect for her chest? Her mama consistently covered herself, but even under her clothes, she appeared thin and shrunken compared to Clara.

"You are making a mess, Clara," Alicia said, sighing. "We need to talk with Sparrow's mama. When will she be back?" Alicia served herself and Sparrow a cup of water each and then picked up her sister's cast-off gowns.

"Sparrow's mama is away visiting a sick woman. She is preparing special ointments and teas for the woman, just like her grandma used to do. Remember?" Clara said.

"Sparrow, did you know Clara and I grew up with your mama?" Aunt Alicia dropped the comment casually. Was that old friendship the reason Sparrow and Mama could live next to the hacienda? "I'll tell you about it someday, when we have more time." Alicia turned back to Clara. "Any of these gowns will do."

"Any? Not any dress will do when the French and the American envoys attend my party this Saturday with their top officers. It won't just be our gray-haired governor in uniform. These younger officers deserve to enjoy genuine beauty. I'll wear the blue dress, and you can wear the green one, sister."

Clara's mention of Governor Alvarado caught Sparrow's attention. "The governor will be here?" Sparrow stepped farther into the room, the hand holding her cup of water trembling. "And foreign officers, too?"

"Yes, you silly girl. It would not be a party without all the most important people," Clara said as she stepped behind Sparrow. "Well, look at you. When did you fill out, young lady? You need to try on one of these dresses—put on the pink one." Clara held the dress up to Sparrow's shoulders.

"No, I can't," Sparrow said, backing away.

Clara ignored Sparrow's resistance. "I'll discuss this with your mama. I don't want you serving at my party in that tired apron."

"We must talk..." Sparrow turned to Aunt Alicia, wishing she had spoken about Papa's plans earlier. Why had she waited so long? She looked toward the trunk, and then rethought her situation. Mama always said, *to form a wise decision; look north, south, east, and west.* As Clara went to toss the pink dress into the trunk, Sparrow said, "No, wait, maybe I can try it on."

Sparrow reconsidered her possibilities. She kept this secret for Papa, and so far, she had resisted telling Josefina or anyone. There must be a reason. Sister Placida did not know about Papa's plans and did not suspect Sparrow had a secret. Clara had said the governor and foreign officers were attending her party on Saturday at the hacienda. Then, Sparrow realized she could save Governor Alvarado and keep Papa from getting into trouble at the same time.

"What mischief are you cooking up?" Clara looked at Sparrow as if she suspected she was hiding something, then gave her the pink dress. "Be quick about it. I'll need your help on Saturday night. Many powerful men will attend." Clara repacked her trunk.

"Never you mind about Clara and her so-called powerful men. I remember when I met Sergeant Valdez, he was a lowly private. Now look at him." Alicia and Sparrow moved to the shady seat in the courtyard where Alicia regularly met with her beau, Sergeant Valdez. The yellow birds chirped in their cages, and the sweet aromas of fragrant flowers permeated the air.

"Some girls at school wonder why you two haven't married." Adults were a mystery to Sparrow.

"He has his work with the government, and I have mine at the school. There will be time for all that." Neither Aunt Alicia's response nor the tranquil setting calmed Sparrow. Her heart pounded as she tried to decide if she should share Papa's secret.

"But what if there's no time? What if everything changes?" Sparrow looked at the birds but imagined she was considering all four directions to determine the best course of action.

"So many worries in such a young head. I know you are excited about the possibility of becoming a nun. Sister Placida's invitation was a genuine compliment to you," Aunt Alicia replied, not knowing what truly worried Sparrow. "Let's just sit here for a while. We can tell your mama together."

Sparrow wrung her hands, her eyes wide with fear.

Alicia plucked one of the nearby blooms, a lilac flower, and pressed it into Sparrow's sweaty palm. "I understand your life is difficult. Growing up is never easy, but joining the nuns' order may be the answer to all your problems."

What was the best alternative to Sparrow to explaining Papa's secret? Would Alicia listen to what she needed to say? In that moment, Sparrow decided. Instead of sharing Papa's news, she would ask Aunt Alicia about a different difficult topic that bothered her. "Who is that new, yellow-haired American girl in class?"

Alicia shifted in her seat, turning her face away from Sparrow. They both knew the answer: Helen was Papa's American daughter, Sparrow's half-sister.

# 07
## Chapter

**Sparrow and Aunt Alicia were** still sitting on the patio when they heard familiar voices raised in an argument—Salvador and Señora Tenorio. Salvador spoke in a tone Sparrow had never heard him use before at the hacienda. Alicia held a finger to her lips, warning Sparrow to keep silent and still on their bench.

"It's getting worse every day. Even that foreign man up the river, Sutter, has his private army harassing the Indians. I know what it is like to work in bondage. Soon he will force his workers to join the Americans and turn on us."

"You worry too much. Governor Alvarado has a plan. Times have changed since you were young. The governor will bring troops to maintain order in Monterey," Señora Tenorio argued with confidence. "We must not alarm the others. Lower your voice."

"If nothing is done, we will lose this home, possibly the country," Salvador replied, standing his ground. "The parliament in Mexico City has never sent troops when we needed them to defend the harbor. All they do is demand more taxes, like every government in history." Salvador huffed angrily. "It's the Americans. They want our land."

"If it's anyone, it's the French. We can deliberate with their captains on Saturday," Señora Tenorio coaxed her husband. "Clara has invited all the foreigners here for a party. Just look at yourself—from a poor immigrant to the position of harbormaster. Believe me, the rancho is safe as long as Clara keeps hosting parties."

"That woman will dance us into oblivion. If she wasn't so popular with the governor, I'm sure he would forget us all together." Salvador heaved a sigh. "Let's go inside, *preciosa*."

"Where is Nina? She was right behind me when we met on the road." Señora Tenorio asked. "I hope she has not stopped to dispense more herbs. We need her here."

Their voices faded as both of them headed toward the hacienda.

Surely, Salvador was aware of Papa's plan, Sparrow thought. She grabbed Alicia's arm and broke her silence.

"Salvador is right." Then Sparrow unloaded her secret in one breath. "It's true that Papa made a plan with the foreigners. I heard him say so this morning. Governor Alvarado is in danger." After releasing her burden, she slouched back on the bench.

"Your papa? You mustn't say such things." Alicia held Sparrow by the shoulders and looked into her eyes. "Who else have you told about this?"

"No one. Today, we learned these words in school: reliable, stalwart, loyal. That means my papa is a traitor. Will Sister Placida still choose me to be a nun when she knows this?" Sparrow's confession opened the gate to her other fears and to her tears.

"She will be fair no matter what your papa does. Just wait here for me, and we will speak to Salvador and Sergeant Valdez. They will decide what's best to do." Alicia reached for a bowl that was under the bench. "Here, take these seeds. The birds are hungry. They like it when you talk to them."

Sparrow watched as Alicia followed in the direction Salvador had gone. How many secrets did the adults keep from her? Had Clara and Alicia really grown up with Mama? Was Salvador really an immigrant? Where had he worked in captivity? When did he first meet Papa?

"Don't be long, please," Sparrow called after Alicia. She pinched seeds from the bowl and reached into the first birdcage, murmuring, "Do you like your little home? It looks so calm and safe."

## Chapter 08

"**Do you think those birds** are going to talk to you?" Mama Nina asked Sparrow as she dragged a satchel of herbs and healing ointments onto the hacienda patio.

"Oh, let me help you, Mama." Sparrow took one look at her mother's slumped shoulders and realized she must never consider leaving her and joining the nuns. She needed to protect Mama from Papa's treachery.

"It was a long walk home. I stopped to gather more acorns for our supplies. Then, with a heavier load, it felt like a longer walk," Mama Nina said.

"Señora Tenorio should have carried something for you." Sparrow lifted the bundle from her mother's arms.

"I was the one who stopped to collect more," Mama Nina said. "The more we have, the more we struggle. You should remember that."

That evening, Sparrow was determined to make her mother comfortable in their cabin. She replaced the herbs and medicines on Mama's shelves. She lined up all the supplies on one side of the cabin. Mama Nina did not know how to write, so Sparrow made notes to identify the jars Mama reused from Señora Tenorio's used jams and precious ointments. On the opposite wall of the cabin was a mat of several blankets where Mama slept.

"Come, use this cot." Sparrow smoothed a blanket for Mama over her own cot. "You will be warmer and more comfortable."

"I like to sleep on the ground, close to the earth," Mama said, lowering herself down slowly and carefully. Sparrow looked across the cabin and repeated the names of the herbs in each jar and their purpose. Mama listened and made corrections. It was a twilight ritual between the mother and daughter before the sun went down and the cabin went dark.

Sparrow prepared a tray with jerky meat and dried fruits for their dinner. She decided not to speak about Papa's secrets or Sister Placida's request for her to become a nun. Instead, while they ate, Sparrow talked about things that would interest Mama, like her favorite places to pick various herbs.

Then, after dark, they were disturbed by Josefina calling from outside the cabin. "Sparrow! My mama wants you to come for cocoa."

"It's too late. My mama is resting." Sparrow wondered why she had been summoned for cocoa at this late hour.

"She wants your mama to bring her special spices to the house," Josefina said, referring to Mama Nina's combination of nutmeg, cayenne, cinnamon, and orange rind, a favorite of the family. They used it in their coffee and cocoa on special occasions. With no questions, Mama Nina rose from her bed. She wrapped herself in her warm shawl and wound a bandana around her gray hair.

"In the corner, under the red cloth," Mama Nina told Sparrow. Sparrow grabbed a small packet and a cloud of cinnamon puffed out of it. They took one step outside and smelled the aromas of Josefina's family dinner. The scent of roasted chicken, steamed corn, and freshly baked bread filled the air.

Josefina grabbed Sparrow's arm and whispered, "We are friends. Why didn't you tell me first?"

Which of her secrets was Josefina referring to? Was she jealous of Sparrow's invitation to become a nun, or was she curious to know about Papa's treachery? When Josefina opened the door, warmth and light rushed out into the cool evening air. The sala was set with a crackling fire, and candles twinkled from the tabletop. A tureen of hot chocolate had been placed in the center of the table with a silver ladle beside it. Everyone in the family was present, even Aunt Clara, wearing another new outfit. Sparrow observed the fine settings and compared this to her plain cabin and meager dinner. "Is it a celebration?" she asked.

Mama Nina dropped a pinch of her spices into the cocoa. Then she rolled up the remaining spices and sat comfortably on the rug.

"Come, sit here, Nina. We have special news." Señora Tenorio grabbed Mama's elbow and pulled her up onto the settee where she sat, her yellow skirt billowing around her. The two women sitting together looked like a salt and pepper set, one woman so bright, and the other so gray.

"We had an exciting invitation today." Aunt Alicia bent forward to speak directly to Mama Nina. "Sparrow is held in high regard by the head teacher, Sister Placida, at our convent school." Sparrow clenched her jaw. She'd wanted to be the one to tell Mama all this news. "She is so good that she has been invited to train as a nun and become a teacher! Isn't that exciting?"

"Bravo! Well done," said Salvador, though he was not a particular fan of the church or the school. Señora Tenorio reached out to squeeze Mama Nina's hand. The others clapped politely, beaming at Sparrow and her mother. Mama Nina took a sip of her cocoa.

"She is only asking, Mama. I don't have to leave you to teach as a nun," Sparrow said, studying her mother's expression. Mama Nina should have been the first, not the last, to hear this news, but the others had taken charge of her news, and now they all cheered enthusiastically.

"Perhaps this is as it should be." Mama Nina put down her cup and caught her daughter's eye. Sparrow understood she was being signaled to come to her mother's side.

"Of course it is. Then it is settled," Salvador said. Then he and the others enjoyed their cocoa while Mama Nina spoke in low tones with Sparrow.

"I have dreamed you are on a hill, teaching, with a bundle of sage in one hand and a book in the other. Every place you go, you leave a mark." Mama's dream imposed on Sparrow's own ideas. So, she decided this was the right time to reveal her own secret about Papa, something no one else knew.

"Wait, everyone, there is more news. My papa is making plans with the foreigners. He is a conspirator against Governor Alvarado," she blurted out. The others gasped.

"Really? Your papa?" This was the type of juicy gossip Josefina lived for. No one ever spoke openly about Sparrow's papa, the trapper named Johnson. Señora Tenorio had proclaimed that he and his American family were not welcome at Rancho Duran.

"Your papa has good reasons for what he does." Mama Nina's voice was firm. She lifted her chin and spoke with a clear sense of pride.

"That's enough, everyone," said Señora Tenorio, taking over the conversation. "Nina, please stay here for a while. We grown-ups have some serious matters to discuss."

"I wish Sergeant Valdez were here." Salvador poured something from a small bottle into his cocoa. Clara extended her cup toward the flask, asking for a few drops.

# Broken Promises

Aunt Alicia nodded and said, "He would know what to do."

"What might he do?" Josefina asked.

"Valdez is an officer. He protects people." Aunt Alicia ushered the girls out of the room. "You girls go off to bed. Sparrow, you can stay in Josefina's room tonight."

"Stay here, inside the hacienda? I want to help. Let us stay up and make a plan." It was Sparrow's news after all. But Aunt Alicia just shook her head and shut the bedroom door behind her.

The adults argued long into the night. Every so often, a voice would be raised, and Sparrow could hear snippets of the conversation.

"Mexico is our country. . ."

". . .traitor."

To Sparrow, it sounded like Salvador and Alicia were worried about what Papa and the Americans planned to do. Clara and Señora Tenorio said they trusted Governor Alvarado to maintain his authority over the territory.

After a while, the girls fell asleep, while the adults continued to discuss Papa's plots in the next room.

## Chapter 09

**Sparrow woke up several times** that night, each time thinking about the choices she had to make.

In the morning, Clara opened the bedroom door, a pair of fancy slippers dangling from her hand.

"Are you sure about this nun business?" Clara approached the bed as Sparrow pulled a sheet up around her shoulders.

"Is it a mistake to take the vow of a novice?" Sparrow asked. "Everyone encouraged me last night."

"If you ask me, you are too young to be making such a serious commitment. My entire life changed when I was your age." Clara sat on the bed. "I was barely sixteen when Alicia and I left Rancho Refugio."

"But you had a family—a mama, papa, and siblings. I have no one but Mama, and she needs me here." Sparrow eyed the pink slippers Clara had laid next to her, and it occurred to her that Clara looked very dressed up for the early morning.

"You have us. It's not like your mama left you or lied to you." Clara seemed to talk about a life she'd had before Monterey.

"The girls will be late for school. Let's go," Aunt Alicia called from the sala, where she and Josefina were finishing breakfast.

"Sparrow is going to stay behind and help me this morning," Clara called back, watching Sparrow closely.

"But Sister Placida will expect her. What do you want her to do?" Josefina's eyes darted between Sparrow and Clara as she stood in the doorway. "We should go to school."

"I'll see you later. I promise." Sparrow didn't know what Clara wanted her to do, but she knew she was tired of taking instructions from everybody. She reached for the pink slippers. She watched Aunt Alicia and Josefina leave, shaking their heads like two old women.

"You won't be sorry, Sparrow. If you really want to protect the governor, trust me." Then Clara smiled and said, "Wait here." She swept from the room and returned moments later with a pile of pink material. "I noticed yesterday that you favor this one."

"I do!" Sparrow stood in her underwear and slipped on the pink gown.

"Here." Clara pulled a silver vial out of her bodice and dabbed Sparrow with perfume. "Doesn't that smell lovely? I'm telling you, the nuns use nothing as lovely as this."

Sparrow wrestled with the buttons on the fancy dress as Clara explained she intended to deliver personal invitations to her party to each of the captains in port. Sparrow pushed her shoulders back and her chest out as she noticed how the dress emphasized her blossoming figure. She puckered her lips and tugged at the low neckline. How quickly Clara had transformed her from an awkward schoolgirl to a young woman. A part of her wanted Papa to see her looking so grown up, but another part worried what Mama would say.

"I should tell Mama that I'm going with you."

"For once, you can see the world you are missing. Why waste your young beauty as a novice?" Clara tied back Sparrow's hair with ribbons and then led her out of the house to a waiting wagon.

"At the dock, hold onto my arm if you wobble in those pink sandals and, for goodness' sake, step around any puddles," Clara said in a hushed tone. Some part of Sparrow understood Clara was nervous about secretly leading her, a younger lady, into a grown-up world.

# Chapter 10

**Sparrow realized she needed to** apologize for misjudging Clara. She'd assumed Clara only cared about her fancy clothes and parties. But now, Clara showed Sparrow exactly how to be a part of saving the territory from the Americans. No other adults gave Sparrow this type of respect.

"I'm glad I'm with you and not in school today." Sparrow and Clara rode in the wagon past the convent school toward the harbor. Sparrow smoothed the ruffles on her dress, feeling grown up. She didn't want to miss whatever was coming next.

"At the dock, we will board a small boat that will take us to that big American ship."

"An American ship?" Sparrow's high-pitched voice revealed her excitement.

Clara waved her hand toward a large vessel anchored in the bay. "I know the captain personally. I've been there before."

Before? Sparrow began to suspect that Clara might be up to no good. Or worse, was she a traitor like Papa? Sparrow had no time to turn back as they were escorted up a ramp on the side of a gigantic, three-tiered wooden ship. The vessel flew a red, white, and blue flag from its mast—the traitors' flag. Sparrow remembered Salvador's remarks about the Americans wanting their land. She relived the words Papa had spoken about getting the governor out of the way. Now she was in the heart of his plot, about to face the enemy, in this fancy pink dress.

Was Aunt Clara really helping to protect Governor Alvarado, or was she a traitor? She was certainly brave and fashionable. Then, Sparrow learned Clara's special talent. She knew how to talk to men.

"Your ship is grand," Clara said to the sailor escorting them up the ramp. "You must have a hardworking crew to maintain it so beautifully."

"Thank you, miss. The *Virginian* carries one hundred twenty strong American men."

"One hundred twenty, my oh my," Clara chattered. Sparrow seized on the information and noted the number. Salvador would want such information.

"Yoo-hoo," sailors called out to the women as they neared the main deck. Sparrow hesitated, but Clara pulled her forward. She had a way of walking like she was waving with her shoulders.

"Smile and give them a little wave, like me." Clara gave a nod of her head and raised her gloved hand in a dainty manner.

Sparrow did the same, and a sailor's voice boomed out, "Ten-hut! Captain on deck!" The men were suddenly silent, and the crowd parted to make space for a large man in a white uniform covered with metals. Sparrow thought he might have been the biggest man she had ever seen. The sailors were of normal size, but their leader stood much taller, with broad shoulders and a fringe of yellow hair peaking from below his hat. His face was deeply tanned, and his eyes were a clear blue. He held his hand out toward Clara.

## Broken Promises

"Welcome aboard, Miss Clara," he said. "Won't you and your companion join me for tea?" His eyes darted from Clara toward his men, who responded by straightening their backs.

"You are too kind, Captain." Clara dipped her chin and lifted her eyes up to meet his. "I told my friend that you are a busy man, but she insisted we come in person to ensure this invitation goes directly into your hands. I would be honored to have you join us at Rancho Duran this Saturday." Clara extended the handwritten invitation, and the captain bowed as he received it.

Sparrow felt like she was watching some sort of drama being enacted, for which she and all the gawking sailors were the audience. She suspected the captain and Clara had known ahead of time exactly what they were going to do and say. It was a big, rehearsed, public show. The only surprise came when Clara introduced Sparrow.

"May I present Miss..." Clara hesitated and did not use Sparrow's real name. "Miss Duran, our able medical assistant." It was hard to tell who was more surprised, the captain or Sparrow. She was too nervous to try a curtsy, so she bent forward like she had seen the mission's priest do before the altar.

"So young and so capable. You are welcome aboard Miss Duran. Or is it Doctor Duran? I'm certain you will find many willing patients among my crew." The captain released a hearty laugh and looked around to see if the crew was smiling.

Sparrow was sure they were making fun of her, and she vowed to get even with the big man. She attempted an awkward curtsy, wobbling in Clara's fancy pink slippers. Then she imagined the head teacher, Sister Placida, witnessing this scene and making notes against Sparrow in her little red notebook.

By the time Sparrow untwisted herself from her curtsy, Clara had taken hold of the captain's arm and walked away. Another man stood before her, lifting his arm to offer help, his brass buttons gleaming in the sun. As she placed her arm on his, she glanced up, up, up at the tall man with a black beard, black hair, and coal-black eyes. Her heart beat furiously. It was the same man who had spoken to Papa about the revolt. He escorted her into the captain's dining room, where Clara was already seated, sipping tea.

During tea—served in blue and white china cups—the American captain was full of polite questions for Clara.

"I am so honored to be on your guest list Miss Clara. Some of the other rancheros treat us like enemies. It is so unfair. You said Alvarado will also attend the party on Saturday?" The captain leaned forward to listen for her answer.

"Oh yes, he attends all Rancho Duran events."

"And his top officers, I imagine?"

"Our sala is not large enough for so many guests. Besides, they stay behind to manage the governor's residence, protect his offices, and keep control of the garrison," Clara said, sounding authoritative. Then she smiled toward the black-bearded man. "But your top officers are certainly welcome."

"Perhaps the men can see your medical clinic at the rancho," Blackbeard said. He sat next to Sparrow. She struggled to maintain a pleasant smile and kept her eyes glued to her tea cup.

"Perhaps," Sparrow repeated. She felt certain she had become someone else.

# 11

## Chapter

"**Sparrow, you've got to act** more friendly," Clara said to her on their way to deliver the second invitation. The women rolled and bobbed on a rough sea in the launch that ferried them to the second ship.

"Friendly? Don't you understand the Americans, the French, and my papa are planning a trap for Governor Alvarado?" Sparrow gulped in air and prayed to not get seasick.

"The way you talk tells me what an ungrateful girl you are. I'll think twice about sharing my best dress with you again." Apparently, Clara had used up all her friendly manners on the captain. "This will be our last stop. Try to be polite."

As they approached the second ship, Sparrow looked up toward the top of the gangplank. The sunlight reflected on the hair of two redheaded sailors staring over the railing—the other two men who had met with Papa about the revolt. Her stomach churned.

"Whose ship is this?" Sparrow asked. The vessel was just as large as the first but not nearly as orderly.

"It's French, you stupid girl," Clara said. Sparrow glanced up and saw a limp flag hanging from the ship's mast. It was faded blue and pale yellow.

"Ahoy there." Sparrow was certain she recognized Papa's voice calling from the main deck. She wrapped her arms around her waist and fell back onto the wooden bench in the small boat. Clara was already moving toward the ramp, waving upward to the sailors overhead. She'd never met Papa Johnson since he'd been banned from Rancho Duran before she came to live there.

"I can't go up there," Sparrow panted, bending down to put her head between her knees. She was horrified that she might have to confront her papa. Not only was she aware of his plans to rebel against the governor, but she now had second thoughts about him seeing her dressed up like a grown lady.

"What do you mean, you can't? We've come all this way. Now stand up."

"I just can't. I'm sick." Sparrow's stomach swirled.

"This is what I get for bringing an immature girl." Clara clutched her handwritten invitation for the captain and walked along the ramp. The sailors cheered just as the Americans had done. Sparrow did not look up, but she kept listening for her papa's voice again. A French officer greeted Clara, whose voice rose an octave and became flirty. Would Papa introduce himself to Clara?

Just then, a surprising sound filled the air above the ship. Musicians began a little tune with flutes and a fiddle. The sailors clapped in time to the music, and the tapping of their feet echoed down to the craft where Sparrow sat curled up in a tight ball. They were dancing above, and she was suffering below.

Sparrow wished to be a spy, not a fool. Hiding below, she needed to gather new information for Salvador. She doubted Clara would try to collect any intelligence to help the Mexican governor. Clara was dancing.

"Take a blanket, miss," the launch pilot said, taking pity on Sparrow. "Look up, you can see the gunpowder barrels." He pointed out the portholes in the lower deck. "Six big guns on each side. Big guns like those could shoot a cannonball way up to the governor's house, I imagine."

Sparrow had taken no notice of this man all day, yet now, it was clear he could provide valuable information. "Is that so? Tell me more." She listened intently to this fellow, who claimed he'd once been on a big Spanish warship, shared many other things. She committed the information to memory to report to Salvador. At last, she had solid information to share about the governor's enemies.

She looked up at the ship in alarm when it occurred to her the Americans might even use the party to attempt their overthrow of the Mexican governor.

# Chapter 12

**It was too late to** go to school by the time Sparrow and Clara returned to Rancho Duran. Sparrow assumed she'd lost her chance to be a novice. But now, she had a way to help defend the governor.

Clara had ignored her on the ride back to the rancho, but now her mean voice reemerged as they entered the hacienda. "Take that dress off carefully. You'll need it for the party."

"I'll serve, but not in this dress." Sparrow hadn't liked the way the sailors looked at her.

"I don't want you to wear it. Someone else does." Clara glared at Sparrow as she removed the dress and fancy slippers. "There was one man, an American, who made me promise to introduce him to the girl in the pink gown at my party." Sparrow stood completely still and said nothing. "He pitied my poor, seasick friend in the boat and wanted to dance with her on Saturday."

"He's probably some old, married sailor—I won't do it." How would she hide from Papa if he showed up looking for the girl in that pink dress?

"You are stubborn and ungrateful. He will be the last man who ever takes notice of you—especially if you become a novice with Sister Placida. Now go run back to your mama where you belong."

The door to Mama Nina and Sparrow's cabin stood open. Mama worked inside, sorting Qwè berries onto little squares of paper. Her back was to the door, but she sensed Sparrow peeking in at her.

"Was it a short day at school?" Mama placed three berries on each piece of paper, then she folded the corners inward to close the packet.

"More berries? Did you go alone to collect them?" Sparrow regretted leaving with Clara. Now she had more secrets about the ships, about seeing Papa, and about the pink frock.

"Not alone. I talked to Grandma Masagawa all day." Sometimes, Mama had mystical spells, during which she imagined receiving advice from dead family members. And, somehow, her mysterious dreams often predicted the future. "We talked about you. She also said we must visit my brothers up north at Sutter's mill."

"I was helping Clara get ready for her party." Sparrow stood alongside her mother and looked down at the berries. Nina now placed five berries, a lethal dose, on the remaining pieces of paper. "Five is too many, Mama."

"Some bad people need five—one dangerous man, in particular."

"Mama, don't say that!" Sparrow reached toward the Qwè berries in alarm.

"No, I do not mean your papa, even though he has broken his promises to us. I speak of another man. My head aches, and I have bad dreams about this wicked man, an American who beats my brothers, Pedro and Flaco. I see them in a dark place, and they write your name. We will visit them soon."

"After the party, I will go with you." In the meantime, Sparrow dared not bother Mama with her own worries.

"I dreamed a deer and her baby are chased by a hungry bear," Mama Nina said, turning to Sparrow. "But they stay safe, together. Like us."

"Of course we are safe together, and we have friends," Sparrow said. Then she added, stretching the truth, "Clara needs me to help at her party. Sister Placida wishes me to teach at the school." Sparrow turned her face away to hide her fears.

"My girl, what do you want?" Mama asked. Then she and Sparrow both paused to listen to the sounds coming from the courtyard. Peeking out from the cabin, Sparrow saw it was Aunt Alicia with Sergeant Valdez, her longtime sweetheart. Their love was obvious, and Sparrow longed to know more about it.

"I want to be certain of who I will be when I grow up," Sparrow told her mother.

"This is not ours to know." Mama Nina glanced out at the couple on the veranda. "But I can tell you something about the past. That man, Valdez, escorted Alicia and Clara to Monterey long ago, when they were your age." Valdez and Alicia sat on the same bench Sparrow and Alicia had sat on two nights before.

The couple's romantic whispers were drowned out by Josefina entering the little cabin and begging for details about Sparrow's day. "There you are. What did you do all day?" The tiny cabin felt crowded with the three women. "These look good." Josefina reached for a berry.

Mama blocked her hand. "Not for girls. This is powerful medicine."

"Wait till you hear who talked to me at school while you were gone with Clara." Then Josefina paused, not wanting to reveal any secrets Sparrow may have kept from her mother.

"It's okay. Mama knows I helped Clara with her party plans all day. Tell me, who talked to you at school?"

"It was that strange girl, Helen. Walk with me so we can talk. Clara intends to put us to work the minute we go inside the hacienda," Josefina said, taking Sparrow's arm in hers.

"Mama?" Sparrow didn't want to leave her mama so soon. She was uneasy about the remaining Qwè berries lying on the open papers.

"You go. And be kind to the new girl, Helen," Mama Nina said.

As they walked, Sparrow and Josefina avoided the side of the patio where Alicia and Valdez sat together, speaking in hushed voices.

"They are not the only ones who have secrets to share. Just wait till I tell you what I learned today," Sparrow said.

"Learned? You weren't even in school today. Sister Placida came looking for you twice. First, listen to my secret." Josefina relished her new gossip. "Helen told me she never knew who her papa was until she got to Monterey. He's some dirty trapper. That's why she brags so much. It's all lies. She wishes some man she calls Captain Fremont was her papa. He brought her and her mama with some other settlers to Monterey."

Sparrow's body stiffened at the mention of her papa. There was no way her friend might understand how much the gossip meant to her. She tried to focus on her own news about the ships and officers and was impatient to pass it on to Salvador.

"I learned things that really matter. I've got to share information about the American and French ships with your papa, Josie, and protect the governor," Sparrow said, looking around as if someone might steal her secrets.

Josefina stopped walking and stared at her friend. "Are you playing at being a spy? What will Sister Placida say when she finds out?"

"This is no game." Sparrow reached out to hold Josefina's shoulders and convince her how serious their situation was. "I think the foreigners are going to try to capture the governor tomorrow night at Clara's party, right here at the hacienda. Your papa must anticipate this."

"If you really need him, he and my mother are spending the evening at the governor's home. Apparently, everyone has secrets except me," Josefina replied, sulking.

"I do have another secret that just the two of us can share," Sparrow said quietly. "It's about Clara's pink dress. Let's go try it on." As they walked back to the hacienda, the two girls glanced toward the lovebirds on their bench. Valdez's dark military uniform with its brass buttons framed his tall, lean body. Alicia's skirt hung down to her ankles, her shawl draped over her shoulders. They were holding hands.

# 13

## Chapter

"**I don't understand. If you** love your papa so much, why are you working to fool him with this pink dress?" The dress did not fit Josefina nearly as well as it fit Sparrow. Josefina had no chest, and her hips were straight. They used hair ribbons to tighten the dress at the waist and pull it up on her shoulders. "Why are you trying to shield the governor from your papa's revolt?"

Sometimes, Josefina did not understand her at all, Sparrow thought. Should she explain to Josefina that Helen's papa and her papa were the same man? The girls continued to fiddle with the dress until they heard Salvador and his wife return to the hacienda in the middle of a heated argument.

"The old man can't be talked out of making his grand appearance here at this damned party. He is in real danger and doesn't see it." Salvador paced around the sala, searching bureau draws, cabinets, and closets, taking out weapons as he found them.

"Don't tell me you think the Americans will try to kidnap him from the party in front of everyone." Señora Tenorio folded her arms across her chest. "Put those guns away."

"I got a message from Sergeant Valdez today. The Mexican troops are getting ready to defend Monterey. I will be ready to help them." Salvador put four pistols on the dining table just as the girls entered the room.

"Your papa and I have serious things to discuss," Señora Tenorio told the girls, waving her hands to shoo them away.

"We have information. She wants to help." Josefina stared at her father's guns before her mama folded the tablecloth up to cover them. "Tell them what you learned today."

Sparrow ignored the guns and the instructions to leave the room. "I went to the American ship with Clara. I saw how many men and guns they have. We've got to stop them," Sparrow shared, considering herself a grown-up and very much a part of this adventure.

"You are just children," Señora Tenorio scolded the girls. "Clara shared all of that with us already. She should not have taken you."

This information surprised Sparrow. Her eyes were wide, and her mouth hung open.

"Do you expect you are the only one who is trying to shield the governor?" Señora Tenorio asked. "Clara is doing her part to stop this rebellion."

Sparrow was dumbfounded to learn that Clara was not a rebel herself. She had done a convincing job, making everyone think she cared only for pretty dresses, decorations, and important guests. Maybe there was more that Sparrow did not see.

"Clara's party may backfire," Sergeant Valdez said, as he and Aunt Alicia entered from the veranda.

Salvador uncovered the guns on the table. "I received your message today, Valdez. We are ready."

"I've just told Alicia what I learned on our patrol to protect our southern boundary," Valdez shared. "Governor Pico in Baja California is sending troops to help us defend Monterey. He wants us to meet him in San Juan Bautista."

Sparrow had misjudged Valdez and Alicia. That'd been no romantic conversation; they had been talking about how to defend the territory.

"We can't just stand by and let them take over." Aunt Alicia stood shoulder to shoulder with Valdez. "How can we help? Everyone wants to do their part to safeguard the governor."

Sparrow was disappointed to not be the sole hero. Was everyone defending Governor Alvarado in their own way? Had Mama sensed this? Was that why she had collected extra Qwè berries? Did Mama plan to serve the poison to the traitors?

# Chapter 14

"**We need more candles on** the hearth. Be sure to light Mother Mary's candle and put it in front," Clara said, giving orders to the hacienda staff and the family on the day of the party.

Sparrow was sitting on the rim of the veranda with her knees pulled toward her chest when Josefina approached, sweeping the patio.

"What are you doing out here? Clara is calling you."

"I'm sure she is. There is always someone giving me orders," Sparrow sighed.

"Everyone is doing their part. Move over so I can sweep that corner." Josefina never questioned the tasks she was given.

"In case you didn't notice, I already did my part. I reported Papa's planned rebellion. I was the one to encounter the American rebels on their ship and bring back crucial information about their sailors and cannons. But everyone here still treats me like a child." Sparrow felt the others wanted to get all the credit for saving the governor, and no one gave her respect for all the information she had gathered.

"Well, the patio is my assignment. Why don't you go into the kitchen where there is a lot to do?" Josefina swept around Sparrow until she moved inside the house.

In the kitchen, Señora Tenorio filled silver trays with savory treats. "This may be the last time we use these silver trays if the Americans have their way and take over this rancho."

"Remember to act normal when the foreigners arrive," Aunt Alicia said as she sprinkled sugarcoated almonds and honey-dipped walnuts on a red platter. "We need something white to display the colors of our Mexican flag." She retrieved a white bowl and filled it with chocolate-coated coffee beans.

"Horses! Come quick," Josefina yelled as she left her assigned post on the balcony and ran inside. "Why are they so early?"

"We're not ready." Clara peered out the window. "It's the governor's carriage." The others crowded near the window.

"Valdez is bringing the governor early. I knew he would come up with some sort of clever plan," Alicia told the other women before rushing out to the edge of the courtyard where the carriage had stopped. Governor Alvarado stumbled out of the coach with Salvador at his side, propping him up.

"Look how he is walking," Sparrow whispered as she stood back from the commotion. "Either he is very weak or he is tipsy." In her opinion, the grown-ups were not doing very well.

"This evening is already going wrong. Who knows what will happen next?" Clara said.

"Tonight is about much more than your silly party. Let's get the governor inside, and quick," Aunt Alicia said.

The early arrival of Governor Alvarado sped everything up, and because no one wanted to embarrass him, they all pretended the celebration was already in full swing. They acted as if there was nothing unusual about starting the gathering in the afternoon or the governor showing up drunk. To add to the confusion in the house, more supplies and staff arrived, and the governor began to sample the brandy.

The baker appeared with a tiered cake, so heavy he swayed back and forth before he set it in the center of the large dining table. Mama Nina entered with her arms full of fresh flowers—red bougainvillea, white lilac, and long green ferns. When she realized the governor was already in the house, she found Sparrow.

"What are you doing? Here, take these." She handed the ferns and flowers to Sparrow and then disappeared.

Sparrow thought it was a ridiculous party. There really was no plan to secure the governor, who rambled on as if this were a formal occasion, with many brandy toasts.

First, he raised his glass to his hosts at Rancho Duran. He went on about their loyalty and prominence in the territory of Alta California. Then he slurred another toast to the Mexican capital, as if those in power there might grant him protection.

*Papa and the rebels might arrive at any time, and the territory will be lost*, Sparrow thought. She stood close to Salvador, who finally stepped up to make a toast that revealed the real reason for the governor's early arrival and the scheme to overcome the traitors.

"To our ally, the Honorable Pio Pico." They all nodded and raised their glasses. Salvador continued. "I interrupt because we must leave at once. Governor Pico is ready to turn over extra men and munitions to protect our Monterey garrison."

"At least someone has a plan," Sparrow muttered to herself.

At that moment, Governor Alvarado wobbled to his feet to make one last toast to the future. Everyone stared at him in disbelief. At any minute, he might be kidnapped, lose his esteemed position, and lose the entire territory unless he was smuggled out the back door to a safe spot away from the approaching American soldiers.

"Our coach is ready in the rear portico, sir." Valdez stepped in to pull the governor out the back door of the hacienda.

# 15

## Chapter

"**Can you believe they planned** all of that just to keep the governor safe? Those adults can be very sneaky." Sparrow was eager to rid herself of the pink dress and accidently ripped a seam while pulling the garment off. "Drat!" She and Josefina had closed themselves in her bedroom to exchange clothes so Papa would not find Sparrow in that pink dress.

"Be careful. Now help me tie this up so it looks like it fits me." Josefina stood shivering in her undergarments, with her school dress and white pinafore strewn at her feet. "Do you think we are going to fool anyone?"

"There is only one person who needs to be fooled—my papa. All he knows is he wants to meet the girl who was wearing this pink dress. But he never saw my face the day I visited the ship." She shuddered at the memory of her father's voice calling down from the deck of the ship. "He won't recognize you, Josefina. Don't worry, there will be a lot of commotion."

"You say that as if you are certain of what is going to happen. So far, nothing is going as we expected." Josefina tugged at the dress as they opened the bedroom door to peek into the sala. "Why did I agree to do this?"

The governor's official coach remained in front of the hacienda as a decoy. Señora Alvarado, the governor's wife, stepped into the sala and began her official hostess duties as the French officers approached the front door.

The girls heard Clara's high-pitched greetings, which sounded enthusiastic. "So delighted you made time for our little festivity." But the girls could see she was nervous.

On the other hand, Señora Tenorio's gracious welcomes gave the party an air of formal dignity. "It is an honor to welcome you to Rancho Duran. Please make yourself comfortable."

They also heard Salvador's deep voice exchanging conversation with the other men arriving. The blending of these voices was like an orchestra warming up before the main concert.

"Who is here? Can you tell?" Josefina asked. The girls were surprised there were actual musical instruments being tuned up. The same group of musicians Sparrow had heard aboard the French vessel assembled themselves on one side of the sala. Then Sparrow noticed two men with red hair—the same two who had plotted with Papa. They entered the sala along with the French captain.

"The French are here." Sparrow grabbed Josefina's white ruffled kitchen cap and pulled it down over her eyebrows. "Wait five minutes before you come out." Then she made her way to the kitchen.

The guests enjoyed the music, refreshments, and other treats. Everyone tapped their toes to the music from the lively musicians. There were gracious comments from the French attendees. The guests were mainly foreigners, but there were a few Mexican residents in attendance. Sparrow took a tray from the kitchen and sat outside on the courtyard bench. She wanted a good vantage point from which to see and hear all the action.

"Where is the governor? We see his carriage out front. I look forward to greeting him." The French captain asked everyone he met about Governor Alvarado.

"He is enjoying a cigar out on the patio, I believe," Salvador said, making an excuse for Governor Alvarado's absence. The captain followed Salvador out to the patio. The two men peered out into the dark evening, but there was no governor in sight. As they turned to reenter the hacienda, they heard more guests approach.

Sparrow also heard a rumble. There were no horses or carriages, just dozens of armed, uniformed American soldiers marching in formation toward the hacienda. The first men to reach the patio surrounded the governor's carriage.

"You can never predict what these Americans will do," the French captain said to Salvador. "An impressive arrival, but not the way we French approach a party."

"Good evening and at ease, men. I trust you are here to enjoy our hospitality and not to practice your maneuvers," Salvador said to the Americans.

The American captain stepped up to the official carriage. "I take it Governor Alvarado is inside. I'll want to have a word with him right away. The war between our two countries has taken a turn in our direction, Señor Tenorio."

"Is that so? Governor Alvarado is out taking a stroll. It seems our brandy cast a spell on him," Salvador said calmly.

"A walk? I thought you said he was out here having a cigar," the Frenchman interjected, clearly annoyed.

"I'm warning you, do not protect the governor, Señor Tenorio." The American captain stood facing Salvador. His officer with the black beard stood nearby with a weapon in his hand. Sparrow sat still on her bench, watching the tensions build. How would Salvador keep things calm? Should she help? Would these soldiers demand to search the house? She took a deep breath, stood, and approached Salvador.

"Miss Clara has asked everyone to come in for the next dance, please." Sparrow made her voice innocent and merry.

"I assume you men have met Miss Clara?" Salvador said.

"Yes!" The American and the French captain, and some of their men, answered with enthusiasm.

"It is hard to resist her charm or her parties. Let's all go inside and greet the lady." As Salvador turned, he winked at Sparrow. She took it as a sign that he approved of her actions and exhaled in relief.

"Come this way for brandy and tequila, gentlemen," Sparrow said, waving her arm in the air. The sailors pushed their way forward to follow her for their drinks. She glimpsed the faces of the other women inside the house, pressed against the windows. They seemed aghast at her boldness, and they looked helpless, wondering which way the evening would proceed.

# 16
## Chapter

**The gay mood at the** party continued as Clara paid attention to each captain and made him her partner on the dance floor. Even Salvador and his wife twirled to the music. The governor's wife danced a few minutes before she sat down, fanning her face. Sparrow circulated among the growing crowd with the silver trays and bowls of sweet treats. The guests were soon satiated with food and drink, all except for that one American officer, the one with the black beard. When he spoke to his captain, the noise in the room quieted.

"Shall I instruct the men to search the rancho, room by room, for Governor Alvarado? We await your orders, sir."

"I am embarrassed to confess you will not find him here." The crowd turned toward the governor's wife, who was thinking on her tired old feet and had the courage to speak up. "Something he ate earlier disagreed with his digestion. I sent him home to recover." The soldiers grumbled, some threatening to begin the search anyway.

"Please, continue to enjoy yourselves." Clara did her best to whip the crowd back into some level of merriment. "I assure you the trays have been replenished with fresh treats. Enjoy!" She made her way toward the grumbling soldiers, and Mama Nina followed her with a tray.

"When did your mama come in?" Josefina asked. She stood next to Sparrow, trying her best to look grown up. So far, no one had taken any notice of her. "What has she got on that tray?"

Sparrow stepped in front of her mother and lifted her tray of Qwè berries. "That tray is too heavy, Mama. I'll do it. I know who needs these berries." Mama nodded and stepped away. Sparrow eyed the redheaded twins, the American captain with all the metals, and his overbearing officer, the man with the black beard.

"Sir, I'm sure you will enjoy these treats. Take only a few. There's not much to go around." Sparrow lowered her chin as she held her tray up toward the man with the black beard. "They are best when washed down with brandy." She knew the combination would slow him down and buy Valdez and Governor Alvarado more time to distance themselves from the hacienda. The officer nibbled from the tray and paid her no mind.

As Sparrow's tray began to empty, she noticed new guests entering, including Papa and his American daughter. She was mortified to have that girl with the yellow curls, Helen, at Rancho Duran. Helen beamed a broad smile around the sala.

"Is that Helen and her papa?" Josefina asked as she approached Sparrow and inspected what treats were left on her tray.

"It is Helen. And that man is my papa, and also hers, if you must know the truth." Sparrow choked back her tears. Josefina's mouth dropped open. They watched as the father and daughter danced in the center of the floor. Papa Johnson didn't notice

Mama Nina, Sparrow, or even the pink dress. Seeing her papa dance with his American daughter broke Sparrow's heart.

By the end of the dance, many men were feeling the effects of the berries. The party began to break up as the musicians played slower and slower tunes. Both the American and French captains were getting drowsy. Even the redheaded French sailors were leaning against each other for support.

"Where is everyone going? What about our arrangements?" Papa Johnson approached each of the conspirators who'd helped plan the rebellion. He had arrived so late that he didn't understand the governor was not even at the rancho. As the French and American captains said early goodnights, Papa stood by himself in the middle of the dance floor.

"What about our strategies? Are you all cowards?" Papa Johnson said. Sparrow had never seen her papa look so confused and defeated. She bit her lip, suddenly feeling ashamed to have revealed his secret plans and afraid she'd made his friends sick with the Qwè berries.

"Look, Papa, it's a girl from my school, Josefina. Her pink dress is so pretty." Helen said, finally recognizing Josefina, who stood across the room.

"A pink dress, you say?" Papa Johnson tried to move toward Josefina, but the men who had gobbled the Qwè berries wobbled around and blocked his way.

Sparrow approached Helen while Papa's back was turned and asked her, "Do you realize who I am?"

"You are from my school, the Native girl. Do you work for these people?" Helen replied, leaning away from Sparrow.

"Is that what you think?" Sparrow whispered back, just as Salvador pushed his way through the remaining soldiers and took the opportunity to create order.

"It appears this party is over for all of you." He escorted Papa Johnson and Helen toward the exit.

"Goodbye, Josefina. Goodbye, girl. I'll see you in school," Helen, unaware of the drama swirling around her, called out and waved goodnight.

Salvador bolted the front door shut after the final stragglers were gone, then turned to the family.

"We did it! The governor is protected." Salvador's voice was hushed but proud. Sparrow hugged Mama, though she was uncertain of their victory. Clara collapsed on the sofa, and Señora Tenorio cleared the table to tidy the house, as if they had just enjoyed a normal Sunday dinner.

"What will happen now?" Even Josefina realized the night's victory was fragile.

Sparrow locked eyes with Salvador, certain of what he was thinking. "They will try to capture the governor again, and we must be ready."

# 17
## Chapter

"**We go. We leave now.**" Mama warmed Sparrow's feet with her hands, then tied a pair of soft moccasins around her ankles. It was the morning after the party and still dark outside. Sparrow had tossed and turned all night, so upset to have seen her papa and Helen dance together. "We travel now."

"Where are we going?" Sparrow wiggled her toes. "These are your moccasins, Mama. What shoes will you wear?" Before last night, Sparrow had wanted to be with her papa. Now, she wanted to get as far from him as possible. "I just want to get away from this place."

"We go to see my brothers in the Sierra." Mama Nina placed a burlap bag on Sparrow's shoulders. "The moccasins will serve you on this journey. Now that you are tall and strong, you can help carry the load. My tough old feet know the trail." Mama opened the cabin door and led Sparrow toward the herbal garden on the hilltop. Sparrow breathed in the aroma of the place, now covered with predawn dew, and knew where they were.

"Did you know the party would turn out that way? Papa brought that girl, and he ignored us," Sparrow said, twisting a long strand of her hair. "Will we ever see him again?"

Mama sighed. "You need to know about your father." She paused, folding her shawl nervously. "He did not want to leave us for that girl you saw last night. His old friend, Fremont, made him leave us. He is paid by his country to bring more Americans to settle on our land. They want the land for the United States. This is the important thing for you to know."

"But this is not the United States, this is our homeland." Sparrow wrapped her arms around her waist and wrestled with her feelings. One part of her still loved Papa, and another part hated his treachery.

"The girl's mother was his school friend, before he became a trapper and came here to Alta California. He did not know he left her with a child."

"You should've never had a baby with him. Where does this leave me?" All the confusion of the night's events and Papa's plot raced through Sparrow's mind. "Talk to me, Mama. I am no longer a child."

"Now is the time to make our spirits strong. No more talk." Mama Nina sat down on her shawl and closed her eyes. She was a keeper of the Sunrise Ceremony, so mother and daughter sat and watched the first pink of the sky peek above the Monterey harbor.

"Does anyone know we are going? How far is it?" Sparrow sat up straight when she heard a low voice greet them.

"*Buenas días.*" Josefina's papa, Salvador Tenorio, walked toward the women. "Are you here to watch the French ship leave?" Salvador pointed toward the harbor, where a ship was pulling away from the dock.

"The sailors are leaving?" Sparrow's heart beat fast. Those two redhead sailors who had plotted with Papa would soon be gone.

# Broken Promises

"Last night's party was too much for them," Salvador replied, hiding a smile with his hand. "They will not be here to help the Americans next time. Their little band can play in someone else's territory." Salvador turned to face Nina and Sparrow. "You two look like you are packed for travel."

"Next time? But the governor is protected now, isn't he?" Sparrow bent down to grab her walking stick. Was he saying there would be another kidnapping attempt?

"Our troubles are far from over. Poor Sergeant Valdez delivered Governor Alvarado to San Juan Bautista then rode all night to come back and share his report." Salvador paused. "It was only a narrow escape last night."

"Aunt Alicia will be pleased to see Sergeant Valdez return." Sparrow blushed, worried her remark had been too forward. "How can I help?"

"Nina, your daughter is very observant," Salvador said.

"I teach her to watch and see. What news did Valdez bring?" Nina continued to watch the departing French ship. "Did he report any bears near the Sierra?"

Salvador and Sparrow stared at Nina, both wide-eyed with surprise. "Oh no, Mama, please," Sparrow said, her face flushed. "Salvador doesn't want to hear about your dreams." Sparrow was committed to helping her Mama visit her brothers, but why did she insist on talking about her dreams with Salvador? He must think Mama was a crazy woman believing in her herbs, magic, and dreams.

But Salvador asked, "Why do you ask about bears, Nina?"

"I told Sparrow my dream about a bear chasing a deer," Nina said. "It is a warning. There was a doe, her baby fawn, and a stag. But the stag was not big enough to defend them because one bear tracked them from the seaside and another bear hunted them from the Sierra."

"Your dream tells the truth. We are trapped. This is the news that Valdez shared with me," Salvador said in a low voice. He pointed out the American ship still anchored in the Monterey harbor. "That is the bear at the seaside. Now we will go find the bear coming from the Sierra." Salvador stood and offered his hand to help Nina stand.

"How do you know where we were going?" Sparrow asked, dragging her stick over the ground.

Nina gave Salvador a little smile. "We are going to hunt bear."

# Chapter 18

**The route from Monterey to** Sutter's mill was crooked and rutted. Sparrow occupied herself by daydreaming until the way became treacherous enough that she had to pay attention. She thought about life as a teacher and nun. Why had she let Clara dress her up like a shameless flirt? She intended to apologize to Sister Placida and hoped she could still become a novice.

Mama Nina asked to stop each day to gather special vines, flowers, and tree bark for her medicine supplies. When Mama stopped to do so on the third day, Sparrow fidgeted restlessly.

"If we stop here, it will take longer to get to your brothers, Mama."

They traveled on, and Mama talked to Salvador about her brothers and how they once stole from the ranchers who hired them as day laborers. She told him about their trial for setting a fire at the mission near Refugio. She recalled their transfer, as prisoners, to Monterey and how she and Sparrow's papa followed them north.

"You only told me they planted the vineyard at Mission Carmel. I've never heard all these other stories." Sparrow leaned closer to Mama to hear the old secrets about her uncles. "When will I be old enough to hear everything? I'm not a little girl anymore."

"You are old enough to know many things now. When Mission Carmel was auctioned by the Mexican government, this man Sutter bought my brothers as laborers from the padres."

"Sutter? I need to learn more about him," Salvador said, then he turned to Sparrow. "Your mother's stories and dreams are important. Her brothers are lucky to have such a loyal sister."

Suddenly, they came upon an old man who was lying face down on the side of the dirt path. "What happened to him?" Sparrow asked, pointing at him.

"Wait." Salvador held up his hand and stopped the horse. "Don't be afraid," he said to the man. Then he lifted the man into the wagon. Salvador looked at Nina. "Help me." Nina examined the bloodied man and tended his wounds. Sparrow leaned as far away as she could and held her hand over her nose.

As Nina tended his wounds, the man mumbled to Salvador, "Stay off this road and hide those two Indian women. Every day there are more prospectors coming out of the Sierra." He rolled to his side and spit up blood. "They think their government has won this land and they are free to take whatever and whoever for their pleasure."

"Do they have a leader?" Salvador asked.

"A surveyor dressed like an officer. They call him Fremont. He fills them with stories and spurs them west." The man gasped for breath. "They seized my ranch, cattle, and family in just one day."

"And what about the man called Sutter?" Salvador asked.

"He helps them. Keep away from this road if you wish to be safe. Use the river." The stranger was weak and let his head fall back. "Ask your Indian woman. She will know the way." The wounded man lay back in the wagon. When he closed his eyes, Sparrow dared to look back at him.

"What was he saying? Who did this to him?" Sparrow asked, keeping her distance but wanting to be a part of the conversation.

Salvador looked at Nina. "What river was he talking about? We don't have a boat."

"He said to go this way." Nina turned the wagon toward a sandy pathway. Soon the brush cleared to an open meadow, where slender streams of smoke curled toward the sky. "Look, Ohlone." Nina reached in her bag, removed a small bundle of dried sage leaves, and held them toward Salvador.

"Light them?" Salvador asked. Nina nodded. How did Mama know all these things? Sparrow strained to see the people Mama called the Ohlone.

"Go toward the smoke in the meadow." The strange man in the wagon opened his eyes and looked toward the smoke trails in the sky. "Those Ohlone will trade with you. They have always been fair with me."

Nina carried the smoldering sage and offered her other hand to Sparrow. Together, they walked across the meadow and approached the figures who watched them come.

"Saleki." Mama said a word Sparrow had never heard. The Ohlone relaxed and came near. Soon, Sparrow was waving to Salvador to bring the wagon forward. The Ohlone recognized the old man, whom they called Sanchez, a local rancher who'd traded with them several times. They inspected Salvador's horse and cart and offered to trade one of their canoes.

Then the Ohlone men led Nina to the shade of an oak tree, where a woman, shaking in pain, lay under a blanket.

"They know your mama is a healer because of the burning sage," Salvador told Sparrow, placing a hand on her shoulder to hold her back.

Upon seeing the wounded woman, Sanchez said, "This is the same treachery I saw at my rancho." Sanchez traded gestures with the men, and it was clear the men who'd raided his rancho were the same men who'd hurt this woman in the meadow. "Wild men, with horses and long guns, came down from the trail in the Sierra."

Nina gently pulled the blanket back to examine the woman's mangled body. A young man sat near, tears streaming down his face, a large stone gripped in his hand. Did he intend to put the woman out of her misery? Sparrow wondered.

"Take this," Nina said. The man let go of the stone and turned his palm upward. "Take it." Mama set five Qwè berries in his hand. He leaned forward and pressed them between the suffering woman's lips, one at a time.

Sparrow held her breath. She watched as the woman trembled. Then her limbs became still, her face softened, and she slept with the ancestors. How did Mama have the courage? How could Sparrow learn to be like her?

Moments later, Sanchez passed a small leather pouch to Nina as she, Sparrow, and Salvador walked away to board the canoe.

"These people want to share their yellow sand with you as a sign of their thanks. It is gold from our river. You take it."

"Yellow sand?" Sparrow asked, wondering about the gifts meaning.

Sanchez hung his head low. "This makes the men who plunder crazy with lust and violence."

"This has great value. You can use it to rebuild your rancho," Salvador said. Sparrow marveled at how something so small, something you could not eat or use as medicine, could have value.

"I will not rebuild here. I will go north, far away from this cursed place." He remained on the riverbank, waving goodbye as Salvador, Nina, and Sparrow got into the canoe.

# 19

## Chapter

**Huge river rocks threatened to** block the small canoe carrying Salvador, Mama Nina, and Sparrow on their journey north. After hearing stories of violence from the man who'd been beaten on the road and witnessing the death of the Ohlone woman, Sparrow's senses remained alert to new dangers. She imagined the overhanging vines threatening her like a hangman's noose. After hours of rowing, a dozen Native men appeared along the riverbank. They bent down and doubled over to claw at the river bottom's sand. The men took cover as soon as they spotted the canoe.

"*Hola*, hello." Salvador called out in two languages to greet the men and show that he was friendly. It appeared that these Indian men were laborers, or maybe slaves. They were skinny, caked with dirt, bruised, and scared. Many had bandaged arms, legs, and heads.

"Pedro, Flaco, Sutter?" Salvador asked them.

"Pedro, Flaco?" Sparrow repeated her uncles' names. "They seem so afraid. Why?" She wondered if her uncles were reduced to the condition of these poor souls. Mama Nina leaned out of the canoe, offering strips of jerky in her open palm. The workers took a step closer. One fellow approached the canoe.

"You go," he said clearly. "Pedro, Flaco." The man nodded his head, signaling he knew the names. "Sutter, danger." He took the jerky from Nina and shared it with the others. Sparrow listened as Salvador and Mama considered the options for going farther. Nina urged Salvador to move the canoe closer to shore.

"Let me out." When the boat was in shallow water, Mama Nina stepped in. "We come with medicines." Mama Nina took the packets she'd intended for Pedro and Flaco from her bag. Her skirts were drenched with icy river water, and she held the herb packets up high. "Come." She waved to the men.

Sparrow recalled a painting at the convent school of John the Baptist wading in the river. That Bible story was peaceful, and the people in it were clean and joyful in the water.

"Your mama is a brave, determined woman, Sparrow," Salvador told her, though he kept a close eye on the men. The haggard workers approached Mama as she applied her herbs and medicines to their wounds and sores. After each man was tended, one packet of herbs remained.

"You take to Pedro and Flaco. Yes?" Mama held out the last medicine packet to the workers. The men nodded. Sparrow wished to remember the scene and ask Sister Placida if Mama would be a saint in her next life.

Salvador sat in the canoe, scribbling on a scrap of paper he'd salvaged from his jacket. Sparrow thought it was a strange time to stop and write. He glanced up to survey the stream and the hills to the east, then he sketched a map of the riverbank. Sparrow watched and tried to imagine what it would be like to have a father like Salvador.

"This looks like the farthest I can travel with you." He gave his page of notes and the map to Sparrow. "You take this and get it to Valdez."

"You want us to go on without you? What is on these pages?" Sparrow asked, studying the papers.

"Valdez will know what to do with it." Salvador gathered his things from the canoe. "I must continue alone into the Sierra to find this man—Fremont."

Sparrow didn't want to admit defeat. "But what about Mama's brothers?"

"There is too much danger here. Just go back down the river, then back to Rancho Duran. I will meet you there." Salvador slung a bag over his shoulder and stepped onto the riverbank. Mama Nina scrambled back into the canoe, dripping wet. Sparrow took over the paddling and discovered that moving the canoe was a lot harder than it appeared.

Mama was worn out. When Sparrow turned to look at her, she saw her mama in a deep sleep, her face turned to the sun. Mama Nina looked older than Sparrow ever remembered seeing her.

It was only when they reached the spot where they'd left the horse and wagon that Mama woke up and started babbling. Her words were jumbled at first. Little by little, she remembered where they were and recalled their journey.

"Stop here and make camp. We can go at sunrise," Nina said. The same Ohlone men lifted their canoe onto the shore. Sparrow had spent only one full day in that canoe, but it seemed much longer. She was overjoyed to step out onto the firm ground and looked forward to a peaceful night's sleep under a fir tree.

At dawn, after the horse was hitched to the cart, Sparrow and Mama traveled alone. The wagon felt spacious. Mama created a resting spot layered with blankets in the back of the cart and immediately went back to sleep. Sparrow held the reins and turned to check on her mother every few hours. At midday, she discovered that Mama was sweating with fever.

# 20
## Chapter

"**Halt! Stop that wagon right** where you are!" A young man stood in the road, pointing a long rifle at Sparrow. He looked just a little older than her. Why was he so close to the hacienda?

"Who goes there?" A slightly older man stepped out from the bushes, tugging at his pants. He had a band of red, white, and blue on his arm. These men spoke like the American sailors. Out of sight, a horse whinnied and snorted. Were the Americans already closing in?

Sparrow looked from man to man, hoping there were no more of them with guns nearby. "Who are you? I've got to keep going."

"We have orders to guard this road. Where are you going?" the young man said.

"What are you guarding it for? My mother is sick. I'm taking her to a doctor." Sparrow tilted her head toward Mama sleeping in the back of the wagon. It was almost the truth. And who were they to try to stop her, anyway?

The older man approached the wagon and reached in toward Mama's blanket. "I've got to inspect this wagon."

"Don't you dare wake her. I wouldn't touch those blankets if I were you. Her fever is terrible," Sparrow warned. The man stepped back.

"You know the road between here and the harbor can be dangerous." The young man softened his expression toward Sparrow and lowered his rifle. "You ought to have a man traveling with you."

"I'm not afraid. I'll get off the road as soon as I can."

"She's just a girl with a sick old woman. Let her go. She doesn't know anything," the older man said. So, this was what the Americans were like, acting as if they had every right to control a road and inspect a wagon.

Sparrow wanted to recall the details about these men, their guns, and their horses. She straightened her shoulders and flicked the reins. The wagon moved forward on the familiar path.

Soon after, Sparrow arrived at the hacienda, where everything was quiet and still. The windows were shut tight, and the curtains were drawn. She got out of the cart and tried the door. It was locked. A curtain on the front window fluttered, and Sparrow recognized Josefina peeking out.

"She's here. Come see!" Josefina screamed when she saw Sparrow. Then the door burst open.

Señora Tenorio rushed out, followed by Aunt Alicia. "We were so worried. Where is Salvador?"

"Where is your mama? Are you all alone?" Aunt Alicia moved closer and saw Mama Nina covered in blankets. "Is she ill? Is she—?"

"Give Sparrow a chance to catch her breath. Someone take the reins," Señora Tenorio interjected, taking charge. Sparrow looked at the anxious faces of the family—her family. For some reason she did not understand, she burst into tears. Was it the men with guns who'd frightened her? Was it Mama's fever and the long, lonely trip home?

"Come in, come in. You must eat and have a hot bath," Señora Tenorio told Sparrow. Then she peered at Mama Nina in the back of the cart. "She does not look well. What happened?"

"I've never known her to sleep so much." Sparrow gulped in air between her words. "I gave her water all along the way, but she has a burning fever." Her legs wobbled. After all she'd witnessed on her short trip north, she was pleased to have the others take charge of her and Mama. When she entered the house, Aunt Alicia brought Sparrow a plate of cold food. It was not what she'd been expecting.

"Sorry, we have so little to share tonight," Aunt Alicia said. "We must hurry." Meanwhile, Señora Tenorio and Josefina pulled bed sheets over the furniture in the sala. Baskets and boxes brimming with the family's belongings were placed near the door.

"What is going on here? Are you traveling somewhere?" Sparrow asked.

"Sparrow, we cannot stop the Americans. Our hacienda is too far from the pueblo to get protection from our Mexican troops." Señora Tenorio placed a hand on Sparrow's shoulder. "Josefina packed a few extra things for you. Join us."

"I don't understand why you are so frightened and running away. Have you no courage and faith in our Mexican armies?" Sparrow raised her voice in challenge. It was a new experience for her.

Señora Tenorio sighed. "The time for resistance is over. We must find shelter."

"Well, I'm not going with you. I'm not running away just because some old men think they can take away our home." Sparrow's outburst surprised the other women.

"You've had a few strenuous days on the road, dear. You will feel better once you get a little rest," Señora Tenorio replied, trying to calm Sparrow.

"You want me to rest at a time like this? Just take care of my mama." The women had situated Nina on the couch. "She has been helping others who were attacked by the invaders." Sparrow focused on her one assignment. "She needs your help, but I am well. I must find Valdez. I have important news for him from Salvador." When Sparrow got up from the table, she realized she now stood eye to eye with Señora Tenorio. When had that happened?

"What news? Why isn't Salvador with you?" Aunt Alicia asked.

"He told me the sooner I find Valdez, the sooner we can stop this American invasion. I will not let my papa's plans succeed."

Suddenly, the front door swung wide open. The women stopped their packing and shrieked, fearing enemy forces were already attacking the house.

Instead, Sister Placida ran inside. "Is Sparrow here? I pray to God she is all right. And Mama Nina?" Then she noticed Nina lying on the sofa. "I would never forgive myself if anything happened to you." The sister was out of breath, and her cheeks were bright red after her dramatic entrance. "I am sorry to make such a fuss."

"We are glad to see you. But right now, we must find a safe place. The times are dangerous. The Americans have already begun to take control of the road to Monterey." Señora Tenorio spoke quickly and pointed to the baskets and boxes. "Let's get these things out to the wagon."

Sparrow's letter lay on top of her pack. "Be careful with that letter," Sparrow said when she saw Josefina examining the papers written in her papa's hand. "Those are private, important, and my responsibility." She wrapped her shawl around her shoulders, prepared to get to Valdez on her own if the others would not help.

"What makes you so bossy?" Josefina said. "I'm just doing what my mama tells me. Do you think you have a better plan?"

Sparrow snatched the letter from Josefina's hands. "Yes, I do." Mama Nina watched the women's interactions from her corner of the sofa. At Sparrow's words, she nodded her head, and her parched lips formed a tiny smile.

"Okay, I'll tell you where Valdez is, but you must not tell anyone," Aunt Alicia said. "I know this much: Governor Alvarado will not return with new troops." Aunt Alicia sighed and hung her head. "This is what Valdez told me. Governor Pico made a deal with the Americans. The Americans promised to make Pico governor of the entire territory if he detained Alvarado. So, he is holding Alvarado and his troops hostage in San Juan Bautista until the American invasion is complete."

Sparrow gasped. Why hadn't Aunt Alicia shared this news earlier? Sparrow's chest grew tight with fear. Who would come to help defend Monterey? How could they defeat the American forces without more Mexican soldiers?

Then Aunt Alicia added, "Valdez is keeping lookout near the harbor."

"Let me take the girls to find Valdez. No one will detain a nun and two girls," Sister Placida said.

"Can I go? I can help," Josefina blurted out. "We can find Valdez together." Josefina moved to Sparrow's side.

"Josie!" Señora Tenorio scolded, and she guarded the door. "And you, Sister, you surprise me. Have you forgotten all your propriety?" The women faced one another, and no one spoke for a few moments. Then, the alliances shifted.

"It is our job to nurse our old friend Nina back to health, Maria Theresa." Aunt Alicia used Señora Tenorio's personal name and pulled her to the couch. "How many times has she cared for us? Let the girls go with the nun."

# Chapter 21

"**Follow me, girls. We need** a few more things, and then we will be the best spies in the Mexican government," Sister Placida said.

Sparrow and Josefina exchanged wide-eyed expressions. At last, Sparrow was being treated like an adult. Sparrow grinned at the nun. She clenched Salvador's map and letter in her fist and felt the urgency of her assignment to find Valdez. The women started toward the harbor to pass on the message.

"Wait. What are we doing here? We've got to locate Valdez," Sparrow protested when Sister Placida made a detour to the school. It'd been shut down because of the political turmoil. Sparrow noticed how small and desolate it looked. "Why does everything look so different?" She entered the classroom and tried to imagine what it would be like to be a teacher.

"I'm taking these with me. What do you want to take?" Josefina didn't seem to notice any difference. She went right to her desk and retrieved her notebook and slate.

Sister Placida unlocked the supply closets that held books, slates, rulers, and maps. "Come back here, girls."

"Hey, look, Josie." Sparrow reached for two plain gowns, the kind worn by the nuns. "Here, pick it up."

"Not me." Josefina watched in horror as Sparrow slipped on a nun's habit.

"No one will stop us if we are dressed like this."

Josefina took a step back. "We were only supposed to collect extra supplies."

"Go ahead, try it on, Josie," the head teacher encouraged Josefina, who hesitated, as if the gown had some magic charm sewn into it. "When you put it on, open this."

Sparrow opened the carton right away. Inside, she found starched white collars, headbands, and headscarves matching the habits. She took out two of each and handed a set to Josefina.

"How does it go on?" Sparrow fumbled with the scarf and collar until they settled into place and her former identity was covered with this religious costume. "You look so funny, Josie. Do I?" Sparrow had never heard Sister Placida laugh before, but today the nun chuckled as she watched the girls struggle in their gowns.

"Sparrow, I never misjudged your intelligence and bravery," Sister Placida said. Before, Sparrow had thought she understood the headmistress, but now she saw a more courageous side of the sister.

There were no mirrors in the school. Neither girl had ever noticed that before. Sparrow recalled one week ago, when Aunt Clara had given her something unusual to wear—that darned pink frock. The fancy attire had been as different from this nun's outfit as anything could be. But the act of disguising herself, trying on a new identity, was very much the same.

"Why are we dressing like this? Is it a sin?" Josefina asked.

"No, we will call it practice." Sister Placida winked at Sparrow and rummaged through her desk to find a few prayer books. "Take one of these and start reading, especially if we meet anyone on the road to the harbor."

Walking in the long gown was no simple task. At first, the girls tripped and giggled their way down the trail that led past the school to the docks. The route was familiar to Sparrow. How many days had she rushed along it, late for school, because she'd spent her time spying on Papa at the docks?

"We need a good vantage point to watch for approaching American ships. Sparrow, what do you suggest?" Sister Placida asked, guessing that Sparrow knew all the best spots to hide. Sparrow pointed toward the cargo crates, the very spot from which she'd overhead her papa planning the revolt with the foreign men. The three of them found low cartons to sit on. They adjusted their habits and prayer books to appear as if they were having regular noonday prayers.

The dock was quiet. Sparrow glanced around the familiar place and spotted a pair of sailors walking with their arms full of bundles that looked like long-barrel firearms.

"Trouble," she whispered. She recognized the black-bearded man, the aide to the American captain. He and another fellow drew closer to where Sister Placida, Josefina, and Sparrow were hiding.

## Chapter 22

"**Good afternoon, Sisters.**" **The sailors** approached the spot where the three women, all looking like nuns, sat reading their prayer books.

"Blessings on you, gentlemen," Sister Placida replied. The men chuckled and exchanged a grin between them. "We are waiting for Mexican ships delivering school supplies. Have you seen any?"

The sailors looked suspicious. "Mexican ships, you say? No, not one." Everyone knew the war between Mexico and the Americans was holding up all shipments. "This may not be the best place for three women alone today, Sisters," Blackbeard said. He stepped closer to get a better look at the two younger nuns. Sparrow and Josefina held their prayer books up close to hide their faces.

"The Lord will protect us. Thank you for your concern. We won't be here much longer," Sister Placida said. Blackbeard continued to stare at Sparrow. She hoped he would not remember where he had seen her face before. She put her head down and shifted away from him, but she could not restrain herself from talking.

"You seem to be burdened with supplies. We wouldn't want to detain you with such a heavy load." Sparrow's heart beat wildly.

The men tugged at the tarp covering the rifles they carried. "You have sharp eyes, Sister. Sometimes it's best not to see too much," Blackbeard said.

"God sees all. I'll leave the watching to him," Sparrow blurted out.

"Maybe tomorrow our ship will come in," Sister Placida said. "Shall we go, Sisters?" She led the girls away, past the men. Sparrow's palms sweated where she clutched her prayer book. Salvador's letter was concealed under the cover.

The girls were still shaken from their encounter with the American sailors when a small pebble dropped from the sky and landed in front of them.

"Valdez," Josefina whispered. "Sometimes that is the signal he gives Alicia when he is near." Then a second pebble fell on their path. Sparrow wondered how Josie knew the couple's secret signals, but her thoughts were interrupted by Sister Placida.

"Walk on, ladies, as if nothing has happened," she said. "We do not want to give those sailors any reason to follow us." She let her red notebook fall from her arm with a thud. "Oh my, look what I've done. Wait a moment for me, will you?" She spoke in a girlish manner and then bent to the ground and whispered, "Valdez?" A third stone tumbled near the women.

"Perhaps we should rest awhile," Sparrow said in a loud, clear tone. "Let's sit in the shade." She led the group off the path to an area hidden from the sailors.

Valdez stood in the shade behind a tree, a big grin on his face. "New recruits, Sister?" He recognized Josefina and Sparrow under their nun disguises right away. "I only have a few moments. Is everyone okay? And Alicia? Where is she?"

The girls looked at Valdez, surprised he was not wearing his military uniform but a tan jacket that seemed to blend in with the trees and bushes. He was unshaven and more disheveled than they had ever seen him.

"Alicia and Señora Tenorio are with Mama, waiting for us at the hacienda," Sparrow said. "I have a message for you from Salvador. He went north, past Sutter's place, to track the man named Fremont. He made you a map." Sparrow faced the other two women as she whispered to Valdez so that anyone seeing them from afar would think the nuns conversed among themselves.

"Salvador is too late. I learned today that Fremont is headed to San Juan Baptiste to build a temporary shelter for his growing troops. Do you realize Pico made a deal with the Americans?"

"We know. How may we help?" Sparrow placed Salvador's message and map under a pile of leaves to her side. "Shall I put this note here? Read it when we leave."

"We don't have time for all this chatter," Sister Placida said, standing unexpectedly. "Give me that message, Sparrow." She flattened the letter on her notebook and pretended to pray aloud right there under the tree, reading Salvador's message in a singsong voice that anyone would mistake for a psalm.

Josefina got on her knees in a pose they'd learned for the holiday tableau. Her hands were pressed together as if she was in prayer. Sparrow followed Josefina's example and kneeled beside her. Sister Placida continued reciting Salvador's note.

*"We are outnumbered, and I fear I may not stop Fremont's advance. I have sketched this map of his route. He has gathered thugs and renegades to do his dirty work. We have seen the cruelty he serves up to the ranchers and Indians in his way. Pray that our family can find some safety. We are surrounded by the invaders and betrayed by Pico.*

*I do not know if we shall meet again in this world, but I am confident we will meet in the next. Salvador."*

"Amen." Sister Placida finished her prayer by making the sign of the cross.

"It is worse than I thought," Valdez whispered from behind the tree.

Just then, Sparrow spotted an American warship, cannons exposed toward Monterey, entering the harbor. "Look up!"

"Can you get back to the school? You must ring the bell. The people in the pueblo need to be warned." Valdez drew his rifle from behind his back. "The Americans are approaching. Go now!"

# Chapter 23

**The old bell at the** convent school hung from a wooden scaffold. Today, it rang to alert the pueblo of danger. It was a call to action, and Sparrow wanted to be the one to ring it.

"Where is the mallet, Sister?"

"There are plenty of rocks. Get some. Do it like this." Soon, all three of them were striking the rim and raising awareness. The residents appeared with weapons, pots, and rakes as they answered the call.

The girls recognized other students and their families coming toward the school. It took some time for the crowd to recognize Sister Placida. Her expression of determination as she struck the bell made Sparrow wonder what, or who, was on her mind. When she beat on the rim of the bell, her headscarf flew up behind her and her face turned beet red. She displayed a passion well beyond the fervor of her preaching.

"Look at that ship approaching!" Some people rushed to the harbor, thinking they could defend themselves against invaders.

Others craned their necks, expecting some visiting dignitary. The crowd lined up along the dock.

A man on horseback came toward the landing and cried out, "They are coming from the east. Armed soldiers—Americans!" It was Salvador, looking desperate and bedraggled. He must have tracked Captain Fremont and his men from the Sierra to the Monterey harbor with his last bit of energy. "Defend yourselves!"

The American ship in the harbor sounded a menacing horn, and dozens of smaller boats filled with soldiers dressed in red, white, and blue uniforms pulled into the dock. From the east side of the pueblo, a line of soldiers in the same uniforms, five men deep, marched in a steady pace toward the crowd trapped on the dock.

One man rode amid the soldiers carrying a flag with the colors of the Americans. As the troops neared the dock, their leader with the flag strode forward as bugles blared. Somehow, Sparrow knew he was Captain John C. Fremont.

"There are so many," Josefina said. She and Sparrow watched from the school as the scene continued to grow more daunting. The great number of troops was impossible to count.

Valdez approached the school from his lookout spot. "There are too many to fight. I've got to stop Salvador. He's done what he can. Now he will need protection," he said. "Take cover inside. I will bring him here."

"Aren't we going to fight?" Sparrow still clutched the rock she'd used to bang the bell.

"This is an ambush. They're coming at us from land and sea. Get inside." Sister Placida opened the school and ushered the girls to the second-floor window, where they could watch the action at the dock unfold. Soon, they heard Valdez and Salvador enter the building and lock the door behind them.

"Is there any food or water here?" Valdez called out.

"We have supplies in the dormitory upstairs. Come watch with us. Thank God you are both safe," Sister Placida said.

Salvador and Valdez, plus the three women, watched as formal pronouncements began. No one was resisting the invaders.

*"Amigos Californios, saludos.* Greetings from *La Casa Blanca de los Estados Unidos. No te preocupan. Estamos aqui en paz."* At the dock, an aide to Fremont introduced his captain with remarks meant to calm the crowd. Their true meaning was clear. The Americans were not there in peace, as he claimed, but to take over.

"I've never heard of a peaceful ambush," Valdez said.

"Or a friendly warship," Salvador added, struggling to keep standing.

Sparrow could not sit still, and she paced around the landing in disbelief. "We can't just give up!" The longer she wore the nun's habit, the more it scratched at her neck.

# 24

## Chapter

"**Traitors! We should have done** more to stop them." Sparrow could not stop herself from blurting out her feelings.

The ominous presence of an American warship in the harbor and the troops on the ground discouraged anyone else from disputing Fremont's pronouncements of victory. American soldiers carried drums strapped to their shoulders. A steady beat made everyone in the crowd anticipate something big was about to happen. Jugs and bottles were shared. Pistols were blasted in celebration. Sparrow watched as American soldiers disarmed the shooters with subtle control.

"Hush! You could make trouble for all of us," Valdez said. "Now is the time to listen, Sparrow. Then we will figure out what we can do."

They were soon joined in the school by Alicia, Mama Nina, and Señora Tenorio.

"Look, Mama." Sparrow had never witnessed such a large gathering—Californios, Americans, soldiers, farmers. "Where are the Native people?" She knew they hid in the shadows or in the hill country, where they could wait out the changes and judge the objectives of these rulers.

At the dock, the Americans continued to make pronouncements. "It is clear to all that the war between the United States and Mexico is over and the Americans are victorious. A peaceful transition is at hand. Today, we begin the process of transforming this neglected territory of Alta California into a peaceful and prosperous land for all under the rule of a new nation," Fremont declared. "We offer friendship over conquest, service over servitude, and progress over poverty."

"It doesn't sound so bad, does it?" Josefina seemed impressed by Fremont's remarks. Half the crowd was already nodding in agreement with Fremont.

"Time will tell us what their true intentions are. Just listen," Valdez said.

"The Honorable Pio Pico, the governor of Baja California, will serve as the civil and military leader for the entire territory during this transition." The crowd murmured and looked at each with anxious glances.

"Where is Governor Alvarado now?" Sparrow asked, remembering his escape from Rancho Duran. It seemed so long ago.

"In the spirit of cooperation, I call on a loyal American, John Johnson, to join me here," Fremont said.

Sparrow heard her father's name and froze in place. "He is being rewarded when he should be punished for his part in this takeover."

"I also ask your local leaders to join our Constitutional Transition Committee: Señor and Señora Tenorio and Clara Ortega," Fremont added. "Today, we raise the new flag of this territory." By now, the crowd at the docks was cheering.

"That's an old trick, getting the conquered to join you." Valdez's words were bitter. Sister Placida remained calm and fingered her rosary beads.

Sparrow's papa, Johnson, stepped out from the crowd and stood next to Fremont. The two men unfurled a flag, sending it up a tall pole for all to see. It featured a huge brown bear as the symbol of the new state.

Sparrow's mama stood with her in the school dormitory, watching from the window with wide eyes. Sparrow remembered her mama's dreams about the bears that hunted the deer and her fawn. Mama held her hands over her mouth and then fell back in a faint.

"Get some water for Mama!" Sparrow fanned her mama's face with her shawl while Sister Placida fetched her some water.

Outside, the racket of the ceremonies continued. The troops performed an impressive drill formation and did maneuvers with their long guns. The drummers and buglers sounded their instruments in marches that led most of the local Californios to follow them with their feet, if not their hearts.

"Both of our papas were called forward, Sparrow. Aren't you proud?" Josefina was taken in by the celebrations and ran downstairs to be among the crowd. Sparrow was not proud of Papa or prepared to think of this day as anything other than a calamity. She remained in the safety of the dormitory to tend to her mama. Her struggles to defend Monterey, to assist Salvador, to aid Valdez, had all failed. She was not clapping or cheering like the crowd below. Sparrow knew there were no Native faces in the crowd, on the dock, on the plaza, or even among the regular vendors who sold their simple goods around pueblo. They had all disappeared. She wondered what hiding place they'd found and if she and Mama should be there with them.

## Chapter 25

**After the new flag was** raised over Monterey, an armed military escort arrived each morning to take Salvador and Señora Tenorio to their Constitutional Transitional Committee meetings. The family inside Rancho Duran was divided over the American takeover.

"They know the path to the meeting house. Why do they need an armed escort?" Valdez did not like to see his friends walking between the American soldiers. He and Alicia were suspicious of the Americans. They retreated to the garden each morning when the escort banged on the front door.

It was well known that Valdez and Alicia did not welcome the bear flag and what it represented. They spent more and more time in the garden with Mama Nina, reminiscing about the old days at Rancho Refugio. Mama Nina was slow to recover after her collapse at the sight of the bear flag, which still haunted her dreams. The house was full of serious talk. Salvador also had his doubts about the new government.

"I can't keep a straight face when I tell the sea captains about the increase in their docking rates. What excuse do they expect me to make up?" Salvador had kept his position as harbormaster, but now he was supervised by the Americans. "It's the same bay, the same dock. Even the ships are the same, but the new government has increased the fees."

Shipping fees were no longer charged against Americans, but the taxes doubled for the French and English trade that entered the port at Monterey. There were constant reports about immigrants streaming into the northern port near Mission Dolores. Pioneer wagons kept coming over the Sierra. All were responding to rumors of gold and quick riches to be made by mining the riverbeds and gullies in this new American territory.

Sparrow was facing her own problems at school. Sister Placida had said, "Since we are *all* citizens now, we will learn about the United States." But Sparrow wondered if that was true. She was certain the American girls were US citizens and thought the Mexican girls and their families could be, too. But what about all the people from her old village? "What about me, and Mama Nina, and Uncle Pedro and Flaco?" she wanted to ask. What about the Native men she'd seen working by the river near Sutter's mill?

"I'm not Mexican, neither is Mama. Where do we go?" Sparrow mumbled to Josefina one day. Something she'd been told after school yesterday bothered her. "Helen said I was from the 'savage tribes.' She read it in a newspaper story. Is that right?" Josefina just shrugged. Sparrow was sure bad things were going to happen to her people. The bear flag scared her. These were not questions she dared to ask in the presence of the American students.

The one hope Sparrow still held was that she had the chance to become a teacher. She'd learned the new government was building a second classroom. Sparrow hoped this would be her first teaching assignment. Then, that dream was destroyed.

"Governor Pico ordered a second classroom for American girls," Sister Placida announced. "Helen Johnson will be the first student, but many girls will join her soon. And there will be an American teacher." Sparrow ground her teeth together every time she heard about Helen, her half sister.

## Chapter 26

"**What can I do, Mama?**" Josefina asked her mother one day as she and Sparrow got ready for school. Josefina was eager to be a part of the change. She'd started sewing a red, white, and blue armband so everyone would know how patriotic she felt toward the Americans. Sparrow was more fearful of the political changes each day.

"Just go to school, like before. I'm sure there will be discussions in your classroom about any changes that will take place." Then Señora Tenorio turned to Sparrow, trying to reassure her. "We have a right to live in peace as the loyal opposition. That is a new phrase you girls should add to your vocabulary list." Sparrow did feel better, until Helen made another smart-aleck remark at school.

"How do you stop a war, Sister?" Josefina asked the first question of the day.

"That's easy. One side wins when everyone on the other side is dead." Helen Johnson didn't even raise her hand before she blurted out her answer. The new American students giggled at her answer. She acted like their leader and entertained them with stupid remarks whenever she liked. Sparrow turned her back to the American girls.

"In the old days, that was true, Helen, but not today." Sister Placida's voice was measured and patient. She didn't pick up her red notebook and write a note about Helen's dumb answer, which is what she would have done if Sparrow had said something similar. Instead, she held up the headline in the Monterey newspaper, the *Californian*. The newspaper was a new feature of the pueblo. Less than half of the original residents in Monterey could read. All the Americans could. The headline read, "Treaty Negotiated."

"This paper is our homework for today," Sister Placida said. Some girls grumbled. "Since we are all citizens of this new country, we should know about these negotiations, these discussions." Another one of those extra words for their vocabulary list—negotiations. Josefina waved her hand again. "Yes, this will be on our exams." Sister Placida knew her question before she asked it.

Josefina's mama, Aunt Alicia, and Valdez helped the girls with their homework about the treaty negotiations that evening after dinner.

"Here are the treaty negotiation proposals, girls." Señora Tenorio shared the actual proposals from the day's Constitutional Transition Committee meeting with the girls. "Most people don't have this copy yet." Sparrow wondered if Papa was sharing the same information with his American daughter. She hoped not. Helen would only use the information to show off and brag.

"Sparrow, are you listening?" Señora Tenorio shook the papers in the air in front of her face. "This part is about citizenship and who qualifies." She picked up several more pages.

"Why are there so many rules?" Josefina leaned over the table to look more closely at the proposals. The handwriting was so crammed on the pages and there were many words she couldn't even read. "Why don't they just say that now we are all Americans, not Mexicans anymore?"

"People want to learn what that means. It's one thing to say the words, but another to appreciate what they mean."

"What do you think it means?" Alicia reached out to hold Sparrow's hand. "Don't you listen to that girl, Helen. Listen to this." Alicia picked up the newspaper and folded it over to a new page. "There's another part of the treaty that says 'the Americans have a sacred trust and obligation to the *Indian* occupants.' That's you, Sparrow." Alicia always put the best face on everything.

"A sacred trust? That sounds like our catechism at church." Those words sounded much better to Sparrow. "What does it mean?" Things were getting more confusing, not clearer. "What happens next?"

"Next, our committee will vote on the rules of the new province. Not everyone agrees, but your papa, Johnson, is one of the members battling for Native rights. Some parts of this treaty will become law, some will not," Señora Tenorio said.

"You should tell the girls that there are some bad things in that treaty. I don't want to be around when they become law." Valdez paced around the room with his hands jammed in his pockets. "For instance, who has the right to own land and who cannot. Who may sell a horse and who cannot. Who gets to punish someone who does something wrong."

"This doesn't help with our homework, does it?" Josefina was looking at Sparrow for support. Sparrow thought there was more to worry about besides a class assignment. But at least her papa was fighting for Native rights.

# Chapter 27

**The very next evening, at** the hacienda, Sparrow shared her news from school. "She called me to the front of the room. I thought I had done something wrong. Instead, she had the other students applaud me." The test on the Treaty of Guadalupe Hidalgo was about the terms and topics the family discussed every night at dinner. Sister Placida was impressed and gave Sparrow the highest grade in her class. Her worries had caused her to study extra hard and earn the best grade she had ever received. She held her test papers above her head and wished she could wave her good marks in Helen's face. She worried so much about Native people under this new American government, she remembered everything Señora Tenorio had shared from the Constitutional Transition Committee.

"Bravo! You are making better progress than our committee, Sparrow," Señora Tenorio said. Everyone at dinner cheered her success.

"We argue on that committee just like I argue here with you, Valdez." Salvador and Valdez laughed. They did not agree on much, but they remained the best of friends. "I'm glad our conversations helped you and Josefina in school."

"This looks like a happy gathering. What are you celebrating?" After weeks of absence, Aunt Clara arrived late for dinner the night of the treaty examination. Alicia welcomed her sister with a hug, and the men stood up from the table and gave her a bow.

"How fancy," Alicia said, fingering Clara's silk blouse. Her own clothes were faded from washing. The women didn't have much new to wear after the taxes were raised, and what they wore needed to be washed often. Everything Clara had on was brand new.

"Welcome home." Señora Tenorio served Clara the last drops of her favorite sherry. "We've missed you and are eager to hear all your news."

"Did you bring any presents?" Josefina asked right away. The adults laughed at her request.

"There's an honest girl. To be truthful, I only brought the news tonight. But wait, I have a little taffy in my bag." Clara handed the girls a piece of candy wrapped in foil paper. "Things look good here. I'm so relieved." Clara gazed at the familiar faces and then at the room and its furnishings.

"We are making ourselves comfortable enough during this transition. But I think each of us misses our friend Governor Alvarado," Señora Tenorio said.

"I forgot how big these rooms are. They will be perfect for the next gathering." Clara walked around the dining room, tugging on drapes, pushing chairs against the wall, and straightening the framed paintings. "It's a good thing I came early to get everything ready."

"I take it a party is in our future. Am I right?" Salvador asked, pouring his own drink and then following behind Clara, who examined the condition of the kitchen and then entered the library.

"We were celebrating Sparrow's excellent marks on her exam about the Treaty of Guadalupe Hidalgo. Do you have news on that topic?" Everyone moved from the table into the library to listen for Clara's response, but she ignored Salvador's question about the treaty.

The sight of Clara planning for a party was nothing unusual. When she scheduled an event, she gave it her full attention. Clara's parties became the family's business. She assigned everyone a job and expected full cooperation.

"I suppose you and Valdez could help me roll up this rug to make a small ballroom in here." Clara whirled in her skirts in the middle of the library. "If we could get rid of these nasty old books, we'd have more room for the musicians. Captain Fremont and the admiral just love a good jig."

"What's a jig?" Sparrow asked Josefina. The girls stood back to see what Clara would do next. Her manners were always unexpected and different from her sister, Alicia.

"It's a kind of dance the Americans do," Josefina said. "I hope she is planning some good refreshments, too."

"Of course you will need to move all of your things out of here," Clara said.

"Out of the library? That's impossible. All of our research for the committee is in here," Señora Tenorio said, shooing everyone out of the library. "The drawing room and dining room should be big enough for any party. I can clear a few things from here." She picked up books, trays, and small items from the dining room.

"Didn't I say? Captain Fremont asked me to host a party here at Rancho Duran to demonstrate the family's support for the new government," Clara said. Everyone stopped where they were and stared at Clara. While the group was frozen in place, Nina came in from the garden, carrying a little sprouted sage plant.

"They grow. I planted seeds under our tree and now they grow. Hello, Clara." Nina held the tender plant near her nose to breathe in the soothing aroma. "Soon, we can make a new blessing on this house."

"We're going to need it," Valdez said.

Aunt Alicia sighed, cringing at the idea of entertaining the Americans. "I knew something bad would happen when Clara came back. You should have given us some warning."

"Why is it so important to invite everyone to Rancho Duran?" Valdez asked. Sparrow worried about the safety of inviting the Americans into the house. She'd overheard stories of renegade soldiers and rugged pioneers who looted Mexican property.

"There's no need to be afraid or angry," Clara said. "After all, I convinced Fremont to let you stay out here in the hacienda as long as you would show your support for the new government." She dusted the rim of the china cabinet with the edge of her shawl. "You know as well as I do that the treaty negotiations are not going well. It will be ages before everything is settled."

"We'll have to make the best of it." Salvador remained calm, but he gazed at the shelf where he kept his firearms and his supply of bullets. "At least we are still a part of the Constitutional Transition Committee. That ought to count for something."

"Don't be so glum. Of course you are still a part of the committee, thanks to me." Clara dusted off her gloves. "Now, about tomorrow night..."

As Clara made plans and gave everyone their duties, Salvador took a pistol from the wall display and handed it to Valdez. "We may need this eventually."

# Chapter 28

"**So, you received the highest** grade on the treaty exam? What good do you think that will do?" While the family was busy discussing party plans for the Americans, Clara led Sparrow toward the patio.

"What do you mean? Everyone else is happy about it. I'm going to be a teacher."

"Don't you understand the danger you are in? That treaty will not protect you or your mama. I am with the Americans all the time. I know the things they are planning." Clara grabbed Sparrow's arms, squeezing till it hurt. "Wake up. I have a proposition that may save your life. I'm trying to help you."

"You are hurting me, Clara, and scaring me, too." Sparrow tried to wiggle away from her grasp. "Just tell me what you are thinking."

"It has to do with this party I am planning. It appears you made a lasting impression on a high-ranking American officer. Do you remember him, the one with a black beard, from the

American ship?" Clara loosened her grip and lowered her voice. Then she brushed her skirt, fluffed her hair, and regained her composure.

"That man with the black beard? He bothered us at the dock. I had to hide my face from him." Sparrow remembered seeing him the day the American warship came into the harbor.

"Don't you want to meet him? It may be your one chance." Clara wanted details. "What did he say? What did you do?"

"He talked to Sister Placida. He thought Josefina and I were nuns." Sparrow smiled, recalling their disguises and the excitement of their mission.

"A nun? I hope you are not serious about that business," Clara said, shaking her head. "Don't you realize this man could protect you no matter what happens? That's what he wants to do."

"I got good marks on my exam. I'm going to be a novice and a teacher." Sparrow kept repeating the things she thought would keep her and her mama safe.

"You've got to realize that you are not a little girl anymore. The Americans have been good to me. They will be good to you, too."

Clara's insistence scared Sparrow. "What does that mean? I know I'm grown."

"It means we can use this party to put you and that American officer together. Can I be any clearer?"

Just then, Aunt Alicia stepped out onto the patio and interrupted the conversation. "You can use the party to do what?" she asked.

"We were having a private conversation, but if you must know, this party will be a public declaration of the household's support for the new government."

"A declaration?"

"You and Valdez continue to resist the treaty in public. Salvador complains about the port tax increases even though he works for the Americans now. Señora Tenorio never socializes with the Americans. I'm the only one representing the family," Clara said, spewing out her complaints.

Aunt Alicia held her sister in a steady gaze. "Sparrow, leave us alone and go find your mama. She'll need help with her plants." Sparrow wanted to hear more. Part of her wanted to wear the pink dress again.

"That's right. Go find your mama. Just remember, you won't always have your mama. Then who will take care of you?" Clara said, her words planting a seed of doubt in Sparrow's mind.

Sparrow was much more relaxed in the garden with her mama, and she was glad to have a moment to think about her conversation with Clara.

"Life brings change, Sparrow." Was Mama recalling her childhood? "When I was a girl, we moved each season, summer and winter. There was always a new camp and new seeds." Nina turned to offer a sage sprout to Sparrow. "You take this one. Watch it grow."

"I remember moving after Papa left us. I wasn't too sad about leaving our leaky tent, only sad that Papa could not be with us anymore," Sparrow said.

"Remember when Señora Tenorio made a home for us in the cabin, and I made medicine for her? It was a good trade." Nina looked like she had more to say. "You can make a good trade, too."

"Me? What have I got to trade? I'll just go along wherever you go." What was Mama was thinking?

"I heard Clara say that black-bearded man wants to trade with you. You can make him a home. Sister Placida wants to trade too, and she'll make you a teacher," Nina said, turning her face away.

"But you told me home is where we are together. That is where I want to be." How did Mama know about all these things?

She didn't dare to ask. Sparrow helped her Mama rise from the garden patch.

"Just wait, things may change." Mama's vague comments exasperated Sparrow.

# Chapter 29

**On the morning of the** party, Clara called out for the family to wake up. She was seated in a wagon next to a handsome man with a full black beard.

"*Despierta familia*—time to get up." She arrived with workers and all their supplies before most of the family had left their beds.

"Clara is already here, girls. Get up and get dressed." Alicia entered the room Josefina and Sparrow shared. "There are many people with her. Try not to speak to any of them."

At that, Sparrow's curiosity was peaked. She raced to the front window for a look at Clara's party preparations.

"I'm glad we got this place picked up last night," Salvador said as he passed. Sparrow paid little attention to the adults, her eyes glued to Clara's wagon and the man who sat next to her.

"It's the big man who talked to Sister Placida on the dock," Josefina said, recognizing the man as well, "the one who was moving the rifles for the Americans." This was the fifth time

Sparrow had seen the man, but it was the first time she had ever seen him smile. He chatted with Clara in the wagon and would be at the door in no time.

"It wouldn't be polite if we didn't at least open the door for them," Sparrow said.

"How sweet of you to welcome us, girls. I was afraid I was too early." Clara looked surprised but pleased to see Sparrow and Josefina. She turned to call out to the workers unloading the wagons. "Put those baskets in the kitchen right away and hang the bunting from the far corner of the porch." There was no mistaking who was in charge of this operation. "Major Baxter, may I introduce my niece, Josefina, and our dear friend Sparrow?"

"Young ladies." Baxter bowed. When he lifted his face, he was looking straight into Sparrow's eyes. "Very pleased to meet you." Sparrow struggled to do a proper curtsy given the major's formal manners.

"I'd like the family to meet Major Baxter as well," said Clara. The girls led Clara and Baxter through the house to the kitchen, where the others waited. "There you are." Clara swept her arm toward Baxter. "Allow me to present—"

"We've met," Salvador interjected, none too friendly. "We know you have a lot of party preparations, so we'll get out of your way."

"Family can never be in the way. Major Baxter, since you know Salvador Tenorio, may I introduce his wife, Maria Theresa, Captain Valdez, his fiancée, my dear sister, Alicia, and of course, Sparrow's mama, Nina?" Everyone turned to face the man with the black beard and nodded a greeting. Nina rubbed her chin and looked at Sparrow. "I will expect you all at the party," Clara continued. "The major extends a special invitation to Sparrow, your star pupil. The Americans know so few, ah, local people."

"Thank you, Major. That will be up to her mama." Señora Tenorio was not smiling.

"But wait. You must allow me to assign soldiers to assist you." In a booming voice that made everyone jump, Baxter called out, "Guards!" Two uniformed men rounded the house, leading their horses. "Make sure this lovely family is safe in their home and wait here until I am back tonight. Adios, until then." He and Clara waved goodbye.

"Who does he think he is?" Salvador said, complaining about the guards and the orders Major Baxter felt free to issue. "What the devil do you think he wants with Sparrow?"

"Let's discuss this later, dear," Señora Tenorio said.

Mama Nina tapped Señora Tenorio on the shoulder. "Sparrow will be ready to go tonight."

"But, Mama, there will be no one my age there. And I don't have any party clothes to wear."

"Let's all calm down and get ready," Alicia said, who was used to seeing Clara stir up trouble. "We'll work things out."

# Chapter 30

"**We have to talk, Sparrow.**" At midday, Alicia and Señora Tenorio found Sparrow in the garden with her mama. "We found this in a box with your name on it. Is it yours?" The women appeared to be worried, and Sparrow did not want to look inside the package they held. Reaching for a corner of the wrapping paper, she pulled it back to find just what she suspected.

"It's Clara's. She had me wear it once and wants me to wear it again tonight." Sparrow blushed at the memory of her grown-up body filling out the pink dress. "She must have slipped it into the sala yesterday."

"She used to dress me up when we were children. Why did she dress you in this?" Alicia asked.

"Why does she want you to go to that party tonight?" Señora Tenorio asked.

Sparrow hung her head in shame. "It's him. He wants me to wear it and come to the party."

"Him? Who are you talking about? Did Clara get you to do something wrong? Has that man hurt you?" Señora Tenorio asked. Sparrow was not sure why the women were ready to accuse Clara of something bad.

"Let's just sit down and talk this over." Alicia led Sparrow to the old patio bench where so many problems were discussed. "Do you want to wear this dress and go? You are old enough to make this decision for yourself." Sparrow appeared to have four mothers. Two called for her to go to the party. The other two called for her to be careful and tell them everything.

"Mama wants me to go. She thinks Clara is doing something good for me." Hadn't Mama said so?

"Does this have anything to do with Major Baxter? He sounded very interested in you attending tonight," Señora Tenorio said, putting the facts together. "Tell us how you know him. How often have you seen him before today?"

Sparrow wished she didn't have to answer. The first time she'd seen Blackbeard—Baxter—had been when he'd plotted the American revolt with Papa at the dock, and she was not supposed to be spying on him.

The second time she'd seen him was when she'd been with Clara aboard the American ship, delivering a party invitation. She'd missed school that day.

The third time had been at the party at Rancho Duran, but she'd kept busy monitoring Papa and his American daughter, Helen, that night.

She'd seen him for the fourth time when she'd been dressed like a nun with Sister Placida at the dock.

By the time she finished explaining all this, Alicia and Señora Tenorio just stared at her. "I didn't realize there was so much about you we didn't know." Señora Tenorio wrung her hands.

"She is a grown girl, a young lady now." Alicia smiled softly and took Sparrow's hand. "I'm sure your mama needs your help. We'll talk later."

Sparrow found her mama in the garden. "You go to that party." Nina spoke the words Sparrow did not want to hear.

"Mama, why do you want me to do that? Señora Tenorio and Alicia are worried about me. They think Clara and that Baxter man may hurt me," Sparrow said, trying to sort out her own feelings.

"My brothers traded me to a trapper, your papa, long ago, when I was your age. Alicia was very mad. She and Clara were sure he was a wicked man. But he wanted to learn Chumash ways. He taught me about new plants. He defended my brothers when they were on trial. We followed them to Monterey. Grandma Masagawa told me to go. Then, we made you, our beautiful Sparrow." Nina's eyes followed the birds flying above the garden. "Now, I will tell you, this man Baxter could protect you if you choose him."

Didn't Mama Nina remember the pain Papa had caused when he'd abandoned them? Sparrow wondered. Nina rose, as if the matter were closed, and collected the plants and herbs in her apron. Sparrow followed Mama back into the hacienda.

# Chapter 31

**Major Baxter lay in wait** in the main room of the hacienda for Sparrow's entrance. He took charge, dressed in a fancy uniform with all his metals on his chest. He made a big show of ushering Salvador, Señora Tenorio, and Sparrow into the crowd that overflowed out onto the patio. The three of them represented the family at the party. The rest of the family stayed out of sight. After all, it was not a Rancho Duran party. It was a command performance ordered by Captain Fremont to demonstrate the Tenorios were devoted to the new government.

"What do you think they are all whispering about?" Salvador asked his wife.

"Wait until you see Sparrow in her pink dress. Promise me you will keep a close eye on her tonight." Señora Tenorio draped a large cape over Sparrow's shoulders to cover her feminine form. Many people recognized Salvador and Señora Tenorio from their work on the Constitutional Transition Committee. The couple shared greetings with individuals to their right and left.

The crowd was curious about the young woman with them. Sparrow twisted her sweaty hands together. When Major Baxter slipped the cape off Sparrow's shoulders, the partygoers gave an audible gasp at her youthful beauty. He led her onto the dance floor.

"Salvador, do something." Señora Tenorio grabbed his arm.

"He is her escort." Salvador glanced around the room decorated for the night's event. "Do you realize this is the same room where we first danced when your father was alive? And now here's Sparrow..."

"What has that got to do with anything? Of course I remember," Señora Tenorio said.

"I cannot stop them from dancing." Salvador looked around at the gawkers. Then he heard a man murmur something that worried him. "Just like Pico, that old fox." Salvador repeated it to his wife.

"What do you think they mean?" she asked.

Sparrow did not know how to dance. Major Baxter guided her around the room and grinned at the other soldiers. Sparrow tried not to resemble a rag doll or a prize goat Baxter had won for himself. After one dance she stood, still dizzy, in the center of the floor, staring at Helen Johnson, who walked directly up to her.

"I remember that pink gown. Josefina wore it at the last party. Does she give you her hand-me-downs?" Sparrow had no response, only a wish to knock the punch out of Helen's hands. "My dress is new. My papa bought it for me," Helen bragged. Baxter stepped up to escort Sparrow to a seat near the wall.

"Punch?" asked a serving girl carrying a silver tray with cups to offer. As she extended the tray to Sparrow, her apron stretched across her pregnant belly. Sparrow could tell from her skin and hair that she was a Native girl. The two of them stared at each other, their dark eyes locked with a thousand questions.

"This is Sally. She works for Governor Pico. I thought you all knew each other. This is my Sparrow," Baxter said, making the introductions. Sparrow winced when he said "my Sparrow."

She whispered to the girl, "Chumash." She guessed their people were not from the same village.

"Salinan," Sally answered in a barely audible tone. "Punch?"

So, there were other girls her age here—Helen, Sally, some Native girls she could see helping to serve, and others who stayed close to Governor Pico. Baxter stepped away while the entire Constitutional Transition Committee, including Salvador, Señora Tenorio, and Sparrow's papa, were recognized by the guests, toasted, and applauded. Soon after, Salvador was at Sparrow's side.

"We've done our part. We can go back to the family now." He extended his hand to help Sparrow out of her chair. "Do you see the girls serving us tonight? That is what Baxter wants to make of you. Some say the American officers compete with Governor Pico and his harem of Native women." Salvador was whispering this warning to Sparrow when Baxter stepped forward to block their departure.

"Leaving so soon?" Baxter's squared shoulders were above Sparrow's face, and he was much taller than Salvador.

"We've had an exhausting day. Please excuse us," Señora Tenorio said. "More committee meetings in the morning, you appreciate."

"My guards tell me there was a magic ceremony here this afternoon. Something to do with burning sage? Be careful, you know the treaty outlaws savage practices," Baxter threatened them. Just then, he was interrupted by Sparrow's American papa, Johnson. His other daughter, Helen, hung on his arm.

"Can I assist you, Baxter? My daughter Helen has been begging to meet you. She knows these folks from the convent school. The Tenorios are a fine family." Papa spoke as if he was a regular visitor at the rancho.

"Johnson, is this your daughter?" Baxter's words caused Sparrow to hold her breath. "What a delightful young lady you have become!" But then she saw that Baxter spoke directly to Helen, whose blonde ringlets bobbed with excitement.

Sparrow stood close to her papa. Her heart beat fast. Would he look at her and say her name after so many months of waiting?

"May I have this dance?" Baxter took Helen's hand, and they twirled off to the center of the dance floor, where he showed her off, too.

"Thank you for stepping in, Johnson. It's been a long time." Was it true that Salvador and Papa Johnson were old friends? Sparrow wondered.

"We must go." Señora Tenorio pulled Sparrow and Salvador away. Sparrow turned to look at her papa, who said nothing but wore a sorrowful expression. She thought she heard him say, "Take her back to her mama."

# Chapter 32

**When Sparrow entered the bedroom,** Josefina wanted to hear about everything that happened. "Papa saved me." Sparrow began with the most important event of the evening. "I am sure he said, 'Take her back to her mama.' He saw Major Baxter being pushy with me. He saw I didn't want to stay with him." Sparrow reimagined the evening through her special filter that reflected her dreams.

"Did he ask you to dance? Did you? Did anyone compliment you on your dress? Are you going to see him again?" Josefina barely stopped to take a breath. Sparrow did not care about the thrill of a dance, or a twirl in a lovely pink dress, or an officer who took her arm.

"And Helen remembered the dress. She said it was old and hers was brand new."

"Helen? What was she doing there? You said no one our age would be at the party. She always has new clothes." Josefina reached for Sparrow's hand. "Did your papa really save you from Major Baxter, or is that just what you imagined?"

"It's true. You can ask your own papa. He witnessed it. Did you realize they were friends?" Sparrow felt better and better each time she relived the moment of Papa doing something to care for her. After all this time, he still cared for her. He did not show it too much in front of Helen. She was such a spoiled girl. Papa remembered Sparrow, and he remembered Mama, too. "Take her back to her mama," he'd said.

"I wish I had been there. I would have told Helen to keep her opinions to herself. All the girls in the American class think they are so smart and special. After all, you got the best test marks on the treaty exam. Remember?" With those words, Sparrow was reminded why Josefina was her best friend. She remembered everything and shared everything she had. The two girls chattered and giggled about the other partygoers, the silly dances, and the scary guards that had lurked around the house earlier that day.

"They reported Mama for magic. How stupid, not to recognize a simple blessing with sage? They are just trying to get us in trouble. And," Sparrow hesitated to add, "they used that word from the treaty—savage. I hate that word."

"But that part of the treaty is not going to pass, right? Mama said the deadlines for voting on the final version are coming soon. She told Aunt Alicia that she and Valdez had to decide if they want to become Americans like the rest of us. What will they do?" Josefina's eyes were drooping with sleepiness, but Sparrow was too excited to sleep. She wanted to stay awake to see what would happen next.

When party was over, Mama Nina slept by the fire in the big house, since their cabin had been ruined by squatters and looters. When Sparrow snuggled up next to her, she whispered, "He saved me. Papa saved me tonight." Sparrow was sure her mama was in a deep sleep, but she wanted to repeat the news again. Then she heard Mama say, "He is still a good man."

## Broken Promises

The next morning at breakfast, Sparrow posed a question to the whole family.

"They call her Sally. Aren't the Salinan people in the hills away from Monterey?" She awoke remembering the young girl who'd served refreshments at the party. So young and so pregnant—Sparrow had not realized it was possible. Someone said she worked for Governor Pico. The soldiers called her Sally. How had she forgotten to tell Josefina about this last night?

"You are right. The Salinan are close to the old Soledad Mission. I'm not surprised that she works for Pico," Valdez said.

"Do we need to talk about this now?" Alicia buttered her toast so hard it snapped in two.

Valdez did not notice how upset she was, and he kept on talking. "She might have been Tongva. Pico was in the south for some time. Or Ohlone, the people north of here. They tell me he picks up Indian girls from every place he passes."

Alicia glared at Valdez. "Please, must we discuss this at breakfast?"

"Someone said the other officers were following his example. Evan Baxter." Salvador spoke up, and Señora Tenorio shot him an angry look.

"If Sally works for him, what does she do, Papa? Just serve refreshments at parties?" Josefina asked.

"Now see what you've done. We are going to be late if we don't hurry. Are the guards here?" The moment Señora Tenorio said this, there was a knock at the front door.

"I hope it's not the two who were here yesterday. They told Major Baxter that Mama was doing some sort of magic." Sparrow remembered how awful she'd felt when they'd used the word *savage*.

"Listen to me, girls. Today is the day we are voting on many parts of the treaty. It's best if we do not talk about some things in front of the guards. Sage burning, citizenship, and Governor

Pico's girls—keep quiet about all these things. Valdez, Alicia, time is running short. You must make a decision about becoming American citizens."

# 33
## Chapter

**Josefina and Sparrow stayed closer** to each other than ever at the convent school. Sparrow worried about all the decisions being made by the Americans as she sat through their lessons about the treaty.

"What if Alicia and Valdez decide they do not want to be American citizens? Will they have to leave?" Josefina asked. Sparrow tried to imagine Rancho Duran without them.

"What if the Native people are not accepted in the treaty? Will Mama and I have to leave you? Where would we go?" Sparrow looked around the classroom to see if she was being watched by the other students. "What if those dumb soldiers arrest Mama for doing magic? How can I protect her?"

During the lunch break, Sparrow noticed Helen looking at her suspiciously. Sparrow promised herself she would not make trouble for Papa by mentioning him in front of his American daughter.

At home, everyone was still upset with Aunt Clara for using the rancho for an American party and pushing Sparrow to be involved with Major Baxter. After a solid week of unwanted attention, Sparrow had made it clear to him that she intended to become a teaching nun, much to his disbelief.

Today, the adults were busy sorting papers and hunting for documents throughout the house. Señora Tenorio emptied drawers full of old paper scraps and tintype photos. Salvador hauled in travel trunks from the barn and sorted their musty contents. Alicia cleaned every inch of her rooms, spreading books and papers across the floor. Mama Nina kept quiet in the garden.

"Here comes trouble," Alicia said as she watched her sister approach the house. "To what do we owe the honor of a visit from the first lady of Monterey?" Alicia criticized Clara about her social life in the capital. Although Clara claimed that her interactions with the Americans were protecting the family, Alicia expressed her doubts.

"News, news, news. I always bring you the latest. Is everyone here?" Clara entered the hacienda, spreading her belongings about—a parasol here, a hat tossed there, gloves, scarfs, and other belongings flung on every available surface. "What are all these piles of paper? The house looks horrid."

"Welcome." Señora Tenorio was more gracious than Alicia. "What news do you bring? I hope Captain Fremont has not declared some new edict." Salvador, Valdez, and the two girls joined the group forming in the dining room.

"Is there anything to drink? What a long, dusty road it is from the pueblo to here. You ought to take a smaller house in town. It would be so much more convenient." Clara said this every time she visited after the American takeover.

"News, Clara, what is it?" Salvador asked, getting right to the point. Josefina brought her aunt lemonade.

"You must have seen the proposal for a land commission. Today Governor Pico received a copy of the US Land

Commission application from Washington DC. It will be published in the *Californian* on Sunday."

"What is it for? This was not on our transition exams at school. How can the land change?" Josefina asked. Sparrow braced herself for more bad news.

"The land does not change, but the people who own it do," Valdez said. "I knew this was coming. What good is it to be a citizen if your land is taken from you?"

Sparrow froze in place. Who would take their land? Would it be like the squatters taking over her cabin?

"All you have to do is show your land grant papers to prove you have a legal title to your land." Clara's words got slower and slower as she began to look around at all the scraps of paper and documents strewn around the house. "You have the documents, right?" she asked, panic rising in her voice.

"That's what we've been doing all week," Salvador said.

Clara started lifting books and notes off the dining room table. "You misplaced those important papers?"

"It's just not here. It's been two generations since my papa confirmed the grant with the government in Mexico," Señora Tenorio said, running out of patience. "No one has ever challenged our family's land before."

"No one had the right to challenge it," Salvador said. Sparrow worried that someone might take the meadow where she and Mama collected herbs.

"No one has that right now. This is absurd," Valdez said.

Sparrow remembered the streams and rivers she'd ridden in the canoe. Were they safe? Josefina and Sparrow listened as the adults' conversation became desperate. Property rights and land grants were not part of their studies, but Sparrow soon realized the whole topic was very important and complicated. It was one more thing to worry about.

## Chapter 34

"**Read it to me again**, Josefina." Sparrow hovered over the latest copy of the newspaper, the *Californian*, while her friend read the headlines. The classroom teacher was absent, and all the girls were chattering about the latest news.

"*Governor Pico accused of using public funds to accumulate female concubines.*" Josefina read the headline for the third time, but neither she nor Sparrow was certain about the meaning of the last word, concubines. "Find the English dictionary," she said.

"Will they deport him like he did to Governor Alvarado?" Sparrow pictured the bevy of Native women who'd surrounded Pico at their last party.

"Listen to this." Helen's shrill voice rang out in the classroom. "One woman manages his calendar, one is his cook, another is his maid, a tailor, a laundress. Maybe he will find you a job, Sparrow." The other girls laughed at her comment.

"Never mind her. Keep reading." Sparrow kept her head down to avoid the jeers of her classmates.

Josefina read on. *"American women, newly arrived in Monterey, witnessed Governor Pico and his so-called staff at a recent social event."* Sparrow recalled the party where she'd met one such poor girl, younger than herself and very pregnant.

"After the event, the American women formed a committee and convinced their husbands to take action against Pico," Josefina said, adding her own comments to the report. "I'll bet the Americans were glad for an excuse to get rid of him."

"I met her. Sally, they called her, because she is from the Salinan people." Sparrow shuddered to remember the small girl with the big belly. "I am ashamed; I was only worried about a dance with Baxter. That poor girl had real problems."

"Does he take advantage of these girls?" Josefina asked.

Helen was not done with her rude comments. "Did he ask *you* to dance, Sparrow?"

Sparrow blushed with shame and anger.

Just then, Sister Placida entered the classroom. "Shameful, isn't it?" The students scurried back to their desks. "What will happen to these girls?"

"Can they come here? Can we help them?" Sparrow asked, imagining a classroom full of Native girls.

"I was considering that very same thing." Sister Placida moved her eyes from Helen to Sparrow. "If only we had enough teachers—the right teachers."

Sparrow's entire class was due to graduate. Each student was anticipating the next steps in their young adult years. Helen bragged openly about going to a finishing school run by the Dominican Sisters in San Francisco. Josefina wanted to follow in her mother's footsteps and advocate for women and girls in the new government. Sparrow was unconvinced she had any opportunity in the territory now ruled by the Americans.

After the school day was over, Sparrow gathered her courage and asked Sister Placida, "Do you think I would be the right teacher for Native girls?"

In answer, Sister Placida opened her book and read her notes about Sparrow.

*"I have seen many flowers bloom, but few as grand as our student, Sparrow. Her attendance has improved and so have her grades. I only wish the territory was more stable. Political changes are coming. I've asked her to consider becoming a novice. She has a gift for leading and for teaching. A career in the convent might protect her from the changes that may come from this new government with a history of harsh treatment of tribal peoples."*

"I still remember wearing the nun's habit that one day at the dock," Sparrow said. She did not look up, but she felt the head teacher watching her.

"It does not matter what we wear, Sparrow. It matters what is in our heart. Recently, I had my doubts about you. Here is what I wrote." The nun opened the book to a new page.

*"I am losing hope that Sparrow will ever become a novice and a teaching nun. Her talents are so needed, especially as we open the school to more Native girls. I've been told that Sparrow was twice seen out of her school clothes and dressed maturely in the presence of some of the foreign men. I fear I did not make our vows of chastity clear to her. I can only hope she is safe. I dare not intervene beyond her mother's care or the guidance of Señora Tenorio. What will Sparrow decide about her future?"*

"Who told you this? I did nothing wrong." Sparrow was embarrassed that someone would have reported seeing her in that pink dress. Josefina would never say such a thing. It must have been Helen. "Are you really going to enroll more Indian girls?"

"I hope we can have more girls learn with us. You would be an excellent teacher, especially since we are losing Alicia from our staff," Sister Placida said, searching Sparrow's expression. "We want you here, Sparrow. We need you." Those were the strongest words the head teacher could have offered Sparrow. Words she had never heard before.

"I will do it. I will begin my training as a novice right after graduation." Sparrow couldn't wait to tell everyone at Rancho Duran that night at dinner. How proud they would be.

"So, now we will begin another chapter in our book."

"I like that, a new chapter." Sparrow imagined the story of her life in one of her schoolbooks. That day, she walked away from school proudly. She was needed at the school. Sister Placida wanted her to be a teacher, a special teacher for other Indian girls. Best of all, she now understood what her future would be. Sparrow decided to share her decision with Mama before she told anyone else.

When Sparrow and Josefina arrived home, Mama was folding her shawl and arranging her sage basket.

"Mama, are you the only one here?" Sparrow asked. "You look busy, like when we prepare to travel." She peered into the basket and remembered their nights together in the cabin, when she would recite the herb names and purposes to learn her mother's healing craft.

"The others have all gone to the American council." Nina slowly removed a bracelet and necklace that had been passed down from her grandmother, Masagawa. "They are having big talks today." She had one ring, abalone, that Sparrow assumed was a gift from Papa Johnson instead of any real wedding ring. She removed the ring and pressed the jewelry into Sparrow's hand. "You take these."

"But they are yours, Mama. Why are you giving them to me?"

"Sparrow! We need to shell the nuts for dinner," Josefina called from the kitchen area. "Come help me."

"I will go work in the garden. You help Josefina now." Nina moved toward the garden, where she spent most of her afternoons. Mama moved toward the sunlight and looked back over her slumped shoulder at Sparrow.

"Josefina can wait. I like being here with you. And I have news to share." It seemed to be the perfect time for Sparrow to share her news.

"I am always with you, wherever you go, Sparrow." Mama's voice was faint, and she smiled as she settled in the sunlight. She closed her eyes against the glare of the light, but she continued talking. "I've had a dream of you with your students—Native students."

"How do you know I agreed to teach? How do you know there will be Native students?"

"Go now. Help Josefina. The two of you remind me of Alicia and me when we were girls. It is good to have a friend." What else did Mama see about the future? Her quiet ways and reassuring presence opened a deep calm in Sparrow's heart.

"I'll be right back," Sparrow said, wanting to hear more of Mama's visions.

# 35

## Chapter

**That evening, as the family** gathered for dinner, Sparrow took a deep breath and shared her news about accepting the position as a novice at the convent school and the plans to enroll more Native students. At the mention of girls from the tribal bands, everyone recalled Sally and the other girls Governor Pico kept under his control. Maybe some of them would become Sparrow's students.

"Wait a minute. We can't go on until your mama is here to enjoy this news." Alicia rose from her chair. "I found an old gold coin on my bed when I got home. It looks like the one we found in a cave when we were girls."

Sparrow held up her hand with Mama's abalone ring. "It's her day to give gifts."

"Why do you think she left the coin for me? I'll go thank her and bring her in for dinner." Alicia headed out to the garden.

The meal was steaming, and Salvador was hungry, so he said grace, including everyone in his prayers even though some were late to the table. Bowls were passed, food served, and the conversations continued.

No one looked up when Alicia tiptoed in and tapped Valdez on the shoulder. He followed her outdoors though it was almost time for their dessert of coffee and *postre*. After a few minutes, Alicia returned, looking pale and serious.

"Sparrow, do you have your mama's sage?" Alicia looked at Señora Tenorio as she spoke and shook her head. "Let's light some tonight for an extra blessing."

"Can we make a graduation blessing?" Josefina wanted to begin the celebrations as soon as possible. Sparrow went to the basket near Mama's folded blanket and picked out a bundle of dried sage leaves. She was not sure why, but her feet were heavy as she walked back to the table and leaned over the candles to light the herb. As the first faint stream of sage vapor rose into the air above the dining room table, Sparrow's eyes filled with tears and the bundle of sage shook in her hand.

"Mama is gone. Her spirit is going up with the sage smoke. Is this true?" Sparrow's body shook all over and her vision blurred, shutting out everything but the smoking sage. A part of her mind was certain Mama was gone, but her heart would not allow this to be true.

"Her spirit has visited you, Sparrow. I found her on the ground behind the tree in the garden. Her fingers were still stroking the soil." Alicia spoke softly, but everyone understood her news. "Valdez is sitting with her now." Alicia held out her hand to stop Señora Tenorio from speaking out and jumping into action. "She is gone. There is nothing to be done. She has been sick, coughing blood in the evenings as she slept here by the fire. She did not want me to share this with anyone, and now her time has come."

"She will need this." Sparrow, still holding the burning sage, walked out to the garden. She was wearing Mama's abalone ring and twisted the gift from her papa on her finger. Mama had tried to warn her by giving her precious gifts like her ring, by folding her shawl and blanket as if she was getting ready to go somewhere far away. Sparrow realized she was expected to carry on the sage tradition and the healing herbs and now teach Native girls after graduation. But none of this seemed important or possible without her mama.

One by one, everyone left the table and followed Sparrow out to the garden. The family stood in a circle around Nina, who was curled on the ground, looking peaceful. Sparrow sat close to her mama, holding the sage, chanting a song she'd learned from Mama long ago.

The sun set at Rancho Duran, and all the talk about dessert, graduation, or anything else ended. Señora Tenorio said a prayer in Spanish. Josefina took the petals from a nearby rosebush and shared them with everyone. Each person had kind words to say as they placed a flower pedal on Mama Nina's head—healer, mother, sister, friend, wisewoman.

"Sister Placida will help us with proper prayers," Alicia said.

"Her brothers need to hear the sad news," Valdez said.

Salvador's words startled Sparrow away from her chant. "Johnson needs to know, too." He was right. Papa had loved Mama when he'd given her this abalone ring and when they'd made her. "We can tell him together, Sparrow," Salvador said.

## Chapter 36

**The day could not begin** without Mama Nina. Only one person truly understood Sparrow. The one person who'd held her hand, taught her chants, helped her find the healing herbs in the woods, and remembered the roots of her own family over the generations. Now, Sparrow was truly alone. The part of herself that Sparrow treasured from Mama, the Indian woman healer, was now gone. She rolled over in bed and cradled her head in her arms.

The sun did not shine in the sky above the rancho. Dark clouds covered the sky, and rolling thunder sounded in the west. Sparrow listened to the raindrops pinging against the roof tiles. Her first thoughts were for Mama's garden and how glad she would be for the water on her plants. Then the image of Mama under the tree, rose petals in her hair, crept into Sparrow's mind.

"Sparrow, it is time. Salvador is ready to go see your papa," Alicia said from the other side of the bedroom door. Sparrow covered her ears and drew her knees up to her chest, curling her body into a ball. She wanted to scream, "Go away!" but all she said was, "I cannot go. Tell him to go without me." After all these days, she longed to speak with Papa, but this was not the way she wanted to renew their relationship. Would he want to see her now that Mama was not there to connect them? "I cannot." She tried to straighten her body and sit up, but she was tangled in the bedcovers. "No, wait," she called out as she struggled to release herself. There was no answer from the other side of the door, just murmurs in the kitchen and the sound of the front door opening and closing against the wind and the rain.

"Lord have mercy, where is she?" It was Sister Placida's voice coming from the kitchen. Sparrow finally untangled herself from the sheets and wrapped herself in Mama's shawl. "The angels are crying with us, Sparrow. I've never seen so much rain, so many tears for your dear mama." Sister Placida, dripping with rainwater, stood in the kitchen. Señora Tenorio, Alicia, Valdez, Josefina, and even Clara sat and stared at the nun. Someone handed her a towel.

"You are wet and cold. Don't get ill," Clara said, tossing a second towel to Sister Placida. Everyone was laughing at the nun who looked like a bird caught under a tent. The laughter was needed to break the spell the grieving night had cast upon them. Soon, hot chocolate and *pan dulce*, sweet rolls, revived their energy and spirits. Sparrow reached for Mama's herb basket and the spices in the red cloth—a stick of *canella*, vanilla, for their cocoa—to ward off the chill.

"Your mama taught you well. You have her gift for healing and strength, Sparrow. That will never leave you," Sister Placida said. "I'm making a note to remember to share this and the other gifts Nina gave to all of us."

As the rain continued, the morning passed with remembrances of Mama's gifts to them, even down to the gold coin left on Alicia's bed as a sign of their days together as girls at Rancho

## Broken Promises

Refugio. There were so many happy memories shared, no other ceremony was needed to bury Mama. Señora Tenorio reminded them that many more people in the pueblo would want to commemorate Nina's passing after all the help she'd rendered to the sick and needy. A simple ceremony was planned following the next Sunday mass.

Sister Placida gave the sermon that day for all the townspeople gathered at the memorial service. It inspired Sparrow to imagine that she might someday share words that offered healing, as well as Mama's healing herbs and medicines.

Sister Placida had helped Sparrow write special words to offer as a healing. "Nina served us with a basin and towel and healing herbs for all. Our Great Spirit expects us to share with everyone," Sparrow said. "The Great Father of my ancestors walked the long trail with my people. He is not just the white man's god, but a healer, like my mama, Nina. They are both here with us today." After Sparrow sat down, the people shared many thanks and stories about the care and kindness Nina had shared. Even Papa Johnson was there to join in the stories. He looked on with pride for Sparrow and spoke to her apart from the group.

"Your Mama and I came to this place to follow her brothers. That is why you were born here in Monterey. We loved the flowers, the herbs, and the birds. We promised to love you, our little Sparrow, and to look after Pedro and Flaco. We visited them regularly until Sutter closed his lands to us. Now, I will return and tell them this news. Please allow me to do this as your papa." Papa's words rebuilt Sparrow's hope that he wanted to share his life with her.

## Chapter 37

**Everything was changing, and everyone** at the hacienda was on the move. Sparrow was torn between her new duties at the convent school and seeing her uncles, Pedro and Flaco, one more time.

"I know you need my help, Sister Placida, with all the new students. But I must respect the family I have left—my uncles." Sparrow intended to travel with Papa Johnson and Salvador to find her uncles at Sutter's mill.

The California territory was changing quickly. There were signs of the newcomers everywhere in the pueblo. They arrived daily by wagon, in boats, and even on foot, each of them clutching a news clipping or postcard advertising California gold. They came from distant places after reading and hearing about the promise of easy riches in the hills and rivers of California.

"The stores are crowded, and prices have skyrocketed," Papa Johnson said as he and Salvador gathered the supplies needed to travel to Sutter's land and find Nina's brothers. "The roads are jammed with treasure-seeking crowds."

There were more smoke fires seen near the hacienda at Rancho Duran. The patio and garden were as far as anyone in the family dared to wander. Squatters and raiders protected tiny plots of land as if they had every right to be there. The week after Mama Nina's memorial mass, Rancho Duran was boarded up in the hope that the family could return to their traditional home once all the land grant papers were filed and approved.

Even Valdez and Alicia planned to leave on a trip to locate the land grant documents to save the Duran land. Everyone knew this meant months of travel for Alicia and Valdez.

"We are definitely not getting married under this government." Valdez wanted a real Mexican wedding. "We could get married when we go to the capital of the Republic of Mexico."

"That's why I will not be teaching at the convent school anymore," Alicia told Sparrow. "I put aside some things for you—just books, boots, and a leather bag."

Clara arrived at the hacienda with empty crates and boxes to convince Señora Tenorio to pack up the hacienda. "You can't stay here, Señora Tenorio. You and Josefina cannot defend Rancho Duran alone against all these squatters and interlopers. Valdez and Alicia will not be here to help you, and Salvador will be on the road with Johnson and Sparrow."

"Just what do you suggest? Someone must stay behind," Señora Tenorio said.

"I have secured rooms for you in the pueblo of Monterey on the top floor of a reception hall I manage for Captain Fremont." Clara still hosted official receptions and meetings for the Americans and their allies. "I know you do not always approve of my methods, but please protect yourself."

Señora Tenorio sighed. "Rooms? I guess we have no choice."

# Chapter 38

**The second journey to find** Pedro and Flaco, Mama's brothers, at Sutter's mill was underway.

"This doesn't look like the newspaper sketches." Sparrow eyed the trenches dug near the river. "These riverbanks were once lush and green." She remembered their last attempt to find Mama's brothers and the poor, ragged men they'd encountered along the way. Sutter lured the workers with elaborate promises, then he broke those promises.

Papa Johnson slid down a muddy slope that dipped toward the cold Sierra waters. "I've seen brochures that advertise the West to gullible pioneers. If they knew how tough it is to mine gold, half of them would stay home."

"Where is the mill, the slues, and sifting boxes?" Salvador studied some human footprints in the dirt. "Sutter bolsters the workforce with men like Pedro and Flaco, guarded each day and locked in drafty sheds by night."

"Mama told me she brought her brothers food and herbs many times before Sutter forbade anyone to trespass on his land," Sparrow said, taking big strides to kept up with her papa and Salvador. "The last we heard, Pedro and Flaco were injured and kept locked up as craft laborers. We've got to find the workers' shed."

"We've got to find it and then get past the locks and the guards." Salvador was losing his enthusiasm for the hunt. "You said we were going to visit your uncles, not storm Sutter's operations."

"I should have brought more ammunition and left you in some safe place, Sparrow," Papa Johnson said, giving her a worried look and clutching his revolver. "Sutter and Fremont have been working together to take everything they can out of this land."

Suddenly, the bushes to the right of Sparrow rustled. Papa Johnson raised his gun. "Stop here!"

A feeble arm appeared from the bushes and reached out toward Sparrow. "*Alto, perdido*, stop, danger," a low voice said.

"*Amigo, comida?*" Sparrow replied in Spanish with an offer of food. "Pedro. Flaco." She added her uncle's names, hoping they would be recognized. The arm reached out again, followed by a ragged head of gray hair. The man waved them toward his bush, and they followed.

Salvador approached the man. "He doesn't look too ferocious." Papa Johnson held Sparrow back. "Pedro, Flaco?" Salvador could see what had once been a grown Indian man, now slumped over from hard labor at Sutter's mill. The bedraggled worker tilted his head and pointed behind him. After a few more steps, they could see the low roofline of a laborers' shed, and all three moved toward it.

Their guide crouched outside and spoke again. "Pedro, Flaco." He turned his head side to side and made an unmistakable gesture. He dragged his knobby finger across his neck, indicating death. "Pedro, Flaco."

"Let's get out of here." Salvador readied himself for a quick exit. "I'm sorry, but we've got to leave while we have time. Your uncles are not here anymore, Sparrow."

"Please, just a few moments. I want to see the place where..." Sparrow did not finish her sentence. The guide nodded as if he understood her request and turned to move into the shed. The old man's back was covered in scars. Sparrow and Papa Johnson followed. Salvador waited outside as a lookout.

Inside the shed, the old man led Sparrow to a corner piled with dirty straw, bits of rags, and scrapes of old, dry rabbit skins. Sparrow pinched her nose, trying to avoid the stale air and squalid conditions. Two dozen men squatted on mats, their clothes ragged and their cheeks sunken. How long had Pedro and Flaco suffered in these conditions? Sparrow thought of her uncles as pranksters, the way she remembered them from her childhood. Even in their servitude to Sutter, she imagined they'd found a way to evade the rules, skim some gain, and live beyond his punishments.

"Let's be quick with this. They are not here." Papa Johnson kept an eye on the opening at the dim end of the shed. "They say Sutter's men take quick action against intruders."

"What's over there?" Sparrow pointed to a filthy blanket on the edge of the straw pile. "Grab a corner." She glanced toward their guide as she reached for the covering. Under the woolen wrap lay the scraps of her uncles' work for Sutter—a crude, wooden mallet, a leather pouch, and a pair of handmade shoes.

"*Los hermanos hacian zapatos.*" The old guide nodded and pointed to his tattered foot coverings. Half the workers in the shed wore the same mangled foot coverings made by Pedro and Flaco. They were almost unrecognizable from the new, smooth pair that lay under the blanket. "For you," the old guide said.

Barking dogs and men's voices speaking English could be heard approaching the shed—not Natives or Mexicans, but Sutter's guards. Sparrow reached for the shoes, shoved the small pouch in her pocket, and then took hold of the mallet like a weapon. Papa Johnson held his revolver.

"*Vamanos alla!*" Their guide stepped aside to loosen a wooden panel. He pushed them through, and they were out of the shed and into the open air.

# Chapter 39

**Papa Johnson tapped the mallet** in Sparrow's grip. "What were you going to do with that?"

"I just want to get back to the school. I've got work to do." Sparrow turned her attention to the path and the few items she clutched in remembrance of her uncles.

"Your little girl has grown up, Johnson," Salvador said as he led the way back.

Papa Johnson reached out and tugged gently on one of Sparrow's braids. "I'm beginning to notice that." The workers' shed was soon far behind them.

Then Papa began another one of his stories. "I was in this part of the country before you were born, Sparrow," he said. "I traded with the Patwin people, who lived among the willows along the river called Sacramento. Where are they now, I wonder?" Spending days with Papa Johnson was a dream come true for Sparrow. The terrain was rough, and the threat of danger ever present, but the joy of Papa's stories and his hand on her shoulder every once in a while was something she would never forget.

"That's no mystery, Johnson. Our Constitutional Transition Committee has already begun to see land changing hands and unlawful grants filed by the commercial interests along this river." Salvador continued to serve on the committee even though he found much of the work discouraging.

"The first people to live here are the last to get a land grant." As Papa Johnson spoke, a woman's voice was heard not far away.

"Help us, please. My son is sick." Sparrow hurried toward the sound of her voice. She located her, off the trail with five children and a broken-down wagon. A boy lay on the ground. "God has heard my prayers. We need your help."

The last thing Sparrow expected to see was a white woman and her children so far from Monterey or any other settlement. What was she doing this far from a pueblo, without her husband or any man to help her? The oldest child, the boy on the ground, was maybe ten years old. The youngest, an infant, was crying somewhere in the broken wagon.

"We will help. Sit down, have some water," Salvador said, trying to comfort the woman.

"Sparrow, can you do something? What would your mother do?" Papa Johnson knew Nina had passed on her healing knowledge to their daughter. "I'll collect the baby."

Sparrow watched her father handle the crying infant until it settled against his chest. She wished she was in his arms, held like that infant. The boy on the ground groaned in pain and gripped his stomach.

Mama's use of the Qwè berry came to mind. Sparrow reached in her bag for the few herbal supplies she had with her. She felt her mama's spirit guiding her hands. Just one berry for the boy, she thought. After a short while, the herbs took effect.

# Broken Promises

"Thank God, he's breathing—and so calm. It's a miracle." The woman was relieved as her son responded to the Qwè berry. Her baby rested peacefully in Papa Johnson's arms. The other three children looked on with vacant, hungry expressions.

Salvador retrieved the meager food supplies he had left and shared them with the distraught family. Then he examined the wagon wheel, which had disconnected from the axle.

"Would you believe I can mend this?" Salvador said. "We'll be here for some time. I'll work and tell you the story of the first wagon I fixed when I was your son's age." After hearing Salvador's story of overcoming many setbacks in his younger years, the woman revealed the sad truth of her circumstances. She and her husband had owned a store beside the river. The pioneer miners had bought everything they had, then talked her husband into a card game as they guzzled the last of his liquor supply. The husband played well, but before the game was over, the ruffians demanded he wager their home, land, and even his wife.

"You are lucky to be alive, from what I hear." Salvador hammered at the wagon axle. "Is your husband near here now?" The woman stroked her boy's head but did not answer.

The boy said, "We hid after Papa lost the card game. There was a fight, and they shot him dead." Sparrow wondered if there was more sorrow that the woman could not bring herself to say.

"You and your mama are safe now. And you have brothers and sisters. We have water and long grass. That's what my mama used to make tea on long journeys." Sparrow glanced toward her papa, and a small smile formed on her lips.

"You have learned your mother's ways, Sparrow, and I am proud of you." Papa Johnson helped her pack up her herbs and ointments.

"What good will it do against such violence? If the Americans will do this to their own kind, will there ever be a place where we Indian people can live in peace?"

"There are Indian schools that are supposed to be safe places. I have seen them in other territories, but the children are separated from their parents and made to learn white ways." Papa Johnson's mention of these schools put a new idea in Sparrow's mind.

The woman and her family traveled with them until noon the next day, to a decent-sized pueblo, San Jose, where others could care for her and the children. She thanked Salvador and Papa Johnson and was especially grateful to Sparrow for healing her son. She took an old family Bible from her wagon.

"We have only one thing of value that was not taken by those men. I want you to have it." From the back of her book, she took a folded paper and handed it to Sparrow. "I plan to leave this territory the first opportunity I have."

Salvador looked over Sparrow's shoulder to examine the paper. "This is too much. It's the land grant to your property. You must guard it."

"I never want to see that land again. This young lady saved my son. My children are the only things important to me now," the woman said.

"Papa, I have something to share, too." Sparrow found the leather pouch her uncles had left behind. Johnson looked inside, his eyes wide, then he nodded at Sparrow.

"We will buy the land grant from you and then you will have the funds you need for your family." Sparrow surprised herself with her quick decision, but a flush of confidence overcame any doubts she had. "You need funds to get to your next destination. Take this, please."

"If this is what you want to do, we can make a legal transfer right here," Salvador said looking at Sparrow with a new level of respect. "Your uncles' gold dust will serve a good purpose."

While in San Jose, they visited the claims office to make the trade. They marked the bottom of the grant with the woman's

## Broken Promises

signature, then Salvador signed as a witness to the transfer. He handed a quill to Sparrow.

"Your signature will make it legal." Sparrow looked at the empty line and wrote her given name, Sparrow Johnson.

As she signed, she noticed the oldest boy rubbing his blistered feet. This family had more pain ahead of them, and she thought of another way to relieve the suffering.

"Try these." Sparrow took off her boots and handed them to him. "They may be too big now, but my mama used to say you need new shoes for new journeys. They will get you to your new destination. Then, pass them on."

# Chapter 40

**Sparrow watched the woman and** her children as they parted ways. "Do you think they will be okay? Where will they end up?" She was herself uncertain about returning to Monterey. "Mama's death is a burden I will carry forever. I know now my uncles, Pedro and Flaco, are also dead because of the changes and misery in our traditional homeland," she said.

Papa Johnson spoke the kind of words Mama might have said. "That family will find their way home. You have helped them."

"You used your mama's skills to heal the boy. It was a miracle that the little sack of gold dust your uncles saved was enough to buy her land grant." Salvador quickened his pace as Rancho Duran came into view.

Sparrow knelt to retie her moccasins. She wondered out loud, "Will the bad things in life always be balanced by something better? It felt so good to be able to help someone in real trouble." She noticed the imprint her shoes made in the dirt. "Do you imagine my uncles were thinking of me when they made this?" Sparrow ran her finger on the letter *s*, etched into the sole of the last pair of shoes her uncles had made. Was this her family legacy—death, separation, and a pair of shoes?

As they approached Rancho Duran, Sparrow could see that foreign men were camped on the property. They were ragged and restless. None of them were in uniform, but all were equipped with pistols.

"Don't look at them and don't give them an excuse to bother us," Salvador said.

For once, they passed through freely, happy to have reached the hacienda.

Señora Tenorio stood up from her packing boxes and called out, "Sparrow, Salvador! We've been so worried about you getting through the squatters' camps."

"You? Worried?" Salvador gave his wife and daughter a hug. "Sparrow did a good thing for a stranded family. She used her healing skills. You should have seen it." Salvador put his arm around Sparrow's shoulders. Once inside, he noticed his desk, stripped of all his papers. He bent to inspect the empty drawers.

"Josefina helped me pack up your things," Señora Tenorio said, giving her daughter a nod of approval.

Josefina reached out to touch her papa's arm. "I threw out those old, tarnished candlesticks."

"You did? Where are they?" Salvador rushed to retrieve the old silver. "Just because something is tarnished doesn't mean we throw it away." Salvador rummaged through the trash. Sparrow felt bad for Josefina and squeezed her hand. She knew what it was like to try to please your papa. "Don't you remember the silver candlesticks I made with the twisted cross?" Salvador found the silly sticks and lit the old candle stubs.

"Yes, I remember the story, but this is no time to be sentimental, dear," Señora Tenorio said.

## Broken Promises

"But it is the perfect time, now that we are all back together." Salvador put the burning candles on the empty table. "This is for all those who have helped us on our way—my old friends Blas and Brother David and our excellent guide, Paciano."

"And for my papa, who built this house, and my old friend Ria, too." Señora Tenorio joined her husband.

Josefina did not want to be left out. She added another candle to the table and lit it. "This is for you, Papa, and everyone who helped you when you were a boy. And for our teacher Sister Placida, who helps kids every day."

Sparrow spotted Mother Mary's candle on top of one of the packing boxes and lit it. "This is for Mama and Grandma Masagawa. For my uncles, too. And you, Papa."

Señora Tenorio interrupted the remembrances, but Sparrow could see she had tears in her eyes. "That is a good way to leave this house and face the future. We really must leave. Clara will be waiting for us in her rooms."

Sparrow looked at the bare walls in the dining room, once decorated with family portraits. The precious vases, usually displayed on the shelves, were wrapped with shawls and shirts and packed away. She did not intend to run away to Clara's rented rooms.

"Excuse me, but I have to make my own plans. I don't see any safe place for Indian people. Between the Americans and the fortune hunters, we are caught in the middle." The convent school was her only hope for doing some good for other Native children. "I need to find Sister Placida right away."

"But Clara's rooms are ready. She may be the only one to come out of this battle safely, even if I do not approve of her ways." Señora Tenorio stood in the doorway, ready to retreat to safety with Josefina.

"Come with us, Sparrow. We'll be together." Josefina, though older than Sparrow, spoke with the voice of an innocent child.

Her parents' protection and fawning, which Sparrow had always envied, left Josefina completely dependent.

"I must go my own way now. I will not forget you." Sparrow stood at her full height and looked down at her friend. The others stared at her.

Then Señora Tenorio made the sign of the cross on her forehead. "I'm telling you, these crazy Americans are taking over everything. Oh, forgive me, Johnson, not all Americans are crazy."

"No need to apologize. You were a good friend to Nina and Sparrow when I was forced to leave them. I am back now and in your debt." Johnson reached for a large trunk in the middle of the room. "Let me load this on the wagon."

"Sparrow, how can you be so stubborn? I owe it to your mama to protect you." Señora Tenorio would not give up.

Papa Johnson stood at Sparrow's back. "I have not been much of a father, but I am here to protect her now." She could feel his strength, and Mama's, in her resolve.

"Sister Placida asked me to work with the nuns and gather Indian children into a classroom of their own." Sparrow recited the words she'd practiced on the return trip from Sutter's mill. She had a plan, yet, she could not look at this family who had always cared for her. "Even the new governor says that such a school is needed. I cannot take shelter with you. My people are suffering."

Then Sparrow rushed away from the rancho, clutching her herbs, to search for Sister Placida.

# 41
## Chapter

**When Sparrow reached the entrance** to the convent school, she heard a lively conversation within.

"My officers are delighted with the Indian school idea. Their wives and children will all need household servants, and the school will be the perfect training ground," the new governor said. He'd wedged himself into a student chair, his belly rubbing against the desk.

"You have hatched a brilliant plan to keep this school functioning, Sister Placida. In the military, we would call it a highly effective maneuver." Captain Fremont strolled around the classroom, inspecting maps and books. "The sooner we can separate the little savages from their parents and get them speaking English, the better for everyone."

Sister Placida offered only a weak response. "The school is meant to improve the students' lives." Sparrow could not believe what she was hearing. Was Sister Placida agreeing with these men? Was the school in jeopardy of closing if she did not go along with their intentions for it?

"Of course. We all care about the children." Clara's voice surprised Sparrow. What was she doing at the school for this meeting? "It is such a warm day, let me pour you both another drink." By the sound of his laughter, the governor had already enjoyed many cups.

Sister Placida looked nervous as she tidied the classroom. When she saw Sparrow standing in the doorway, she rushed to her side.

"Stay silent. Don't say a word," she whispered. Then she turned to the others to make introductions. "Here is our newest teacher, young Sister Sparrow, our novice. The one I told you about, Governor."

"She is also my niece." Clara winked at Sparrow as if they were sharing some secret. It was now clear to Sparrow that she had never been included in all of Clara's secrets.

Sparrow curtsied. "Sorry for being late. I've just returned from Sutter's mill."

"It is a dangerous time for a young lady to be out and about." Captain Fremont fixed his suspicious gaze on Sparrow. The others looked surprised. "Were you alone?"

"I've heard that the roads are dangerous with squatters and the gold-crazed miners." Sister Placida's words of caution held a hint of pride in Sparrow's bravery.

"I brought back new medical herbs. There is bound to be great need." Sparrow kept her comments brief and neutral as she assessed the alliances between the four adults. She looked from one to another, trying to decide who was promoting this plan for training Native students to become domestic workers.

"Medicines? That is quite an accomplishment for a young lady," the governor, said looking her up and down with interest. "Have we met before?"

"She is one of our finest graduates," Sister Placida said. "Her mother had a medical practice." If only they could have seen Mama's old, crooked herb shelves, Sparrow thought.

All Sparrow's high-minded purpose melted as the men toasted their plans and congratulated themselves. When had it been decided to accommodate the American settlers with Native servants? Her courage dwindled by the minute. Was Sister Placida just pretending their school would educate Indian children, and was she agreeing to enslave them to serve the invading government?

"Well, you can count on me to be of assistance with whatever you need, young lady. I am the new man in charge in this territory." The governor struggled to his feet. "Feel free to let me know how I may help you. Your Aunt Clara has many persuasive powers." Then he strutted toward the door.

Sparrow could never agree to be a part of such a school. She could not consent to the type of treatment the Spanish missionaries had once imposed on her own mother. Wasn't there another option?

Sparrow pretended to be humble. "You are too generous." She lowered her eyes, striking a modest pose. "Thank you, Governor. I would never want to bother a man of your importance with my requests."

"You have taught her well, Sister Placida. Imagine a girl of her breeding speaking in such a dignified manner." Upon hearing Captain Fremont's words, which made clear his disregard for Indigenous people, Sparrow squared her shoulders and lifted her chin.

"On the contrary, she has taught me about bravery and long suffering," Sister Placida said, a new expression on her face. Sparrow recognized that same determination she'd witnessed when they rang the bell together to warn to pueblo. It gave her even more courage to propose something outlandish.

"Until our next meeting then," Captain Fremont moved toward the door with the governor. Clara said nothing, but she kept a close eye on Sparrow.

Sparrow took a deep breath. "There is one small request."

The two men stopped and looked back at her.

"Yes, yes, anything my dear." The governor gave a wink in Clara's direction.

"I would be grateful if you would escort me to the claims office. I believe it is on your way. I need to file my land grant in a timely manner. I can think of no better witness to the registration than the governor of the territory."

Clara was the first to react to the news. "Did you say a land grant? Yours?"

"This is a surprise. I'm not sure a girl of your, ah, age can make such a claim." Sparrow knew Captain Fremont was not speaking of her age, but questioning the claim of a Native to own land.

"My uncles left me an inheritance, and my father stands as my partner." The image of the squalid shack that had caged her uncles during their last years flashed in Sparrow's mind. "You know my papa well—he is the former trapper, Johnson. We have both signed the title in front of a witness from the Constitutional Transition Committee."

"Johnson, with the US Surveyor's Office? But he is an American." Fremont had never guessed at their relationship.

"Your father?" Clara asked, clearly trying to picture the man.

"Congratulations on the land grant." Sister Placida could not hide her delight. "He is a very fine man. Will he manage the land while you teach here, Sparrow?"

Sparrow reached out to touch Sister Placida's hand. "I thank you for the invitation to teach here at the convent school, Sister. I remember what you taught us when I was a student: the Lord works in mysterious ways." She was sincere in her respect for the nun and hoped she would understand.

"I'll say," Clara muttered.

"My father will manage the land, and I will run a school that passes on our traditions and teaches herbal medicine to Native children. My land is quite far from Monterey and this convent school."

# Epilogue

**Sparrow walked on the soft** soil, and her shoes made an *s* imprint on the land. Her students held a lively debate as they climbed a slope and gathered traditional herbs for their classes on healing. They shared her old, tattered copy of the treaty agreement as part of their lessons. The pupils argued about the meaning of the document and searched for any provisions for the first peoples, the Native people, in its archaic language.

"You will not find us in that treaty, but I know someone who can assist with our pastures and grazing rights." Sparrow thought of Salvador Tenorio and his wife, Señora Tenorio. "They lost their own land and now they help others to gain land." She recalled their kindness at Rancho Duran and their daughter Josefina, her first friend, who now studied with her mother to write new laws to support women. Salvador and Señora Tenorio made sure Sparrow was kept informed about provisions in the new constitution.

Many old-time residents scrambled to save their land grants, but Sparrow's new property was secured thanks to her care of the widow's son they'd met on their trip to Sutter's mill. Papa Johnson protected the land and the students, hidden from those who continued their cruel practices against the Native people. Sparrow's school thrived in the Sierra foothills, far from Monterey and out of the reach of the Americans who ruled the new state of California.

Some Californios went south across the Mexican border, as did Alicia and Sergeant Valdez. Clara remained in Monterey and wrote the social news section for the *Californian* newspaper. After the war between Mexico and the United States, the Treaty of Guadalupe Hidalgo was finally signed.

"The first drafts of that treaty contained many promises for our people, before our homeland became a state. Then the gold rush, and the newcomers it brought to the territory, changed everything. Many promises were broken," Sparrow told her students.

"There are no guarantees written there." Sparrow remembered Sister Placida and shared more of her words. "We make our way by helping others on this journey."

# Author's Note

**Thank you for reading this** story. *Broken Promises* demonstrates the circumstances of the population in Alta California in the years prior to statehood. Many changes, both positive and negative, occurred after 1850, when this story concludes. Some changes were due to larger interests regarding equal numbers of free and slave states being admitted to the union. Some events were due to long-held prejudices and injustices. The California Indian Museum and Cultural Center (https://cimcc.org), near the location of Sparrow's School for Tradition Healing, tells a more complete history of the people and events, as does the National Museum of the American Indian in Washington DC (https://americanindian.si.edu/).

Let me know how you enjoyed *Broken Promises* by visiting https://anitaperezferguson.com, where you can also learn more about the other two books in this series, *Twisted Cross* and *Golden Secrets*.

See the resources available to readers, students, and teachers in the study guide in the last pages of this book and on my website, https://anitaperezferguson.com.

Remember: "We make our way by helping others on this journey."

# Missions Map

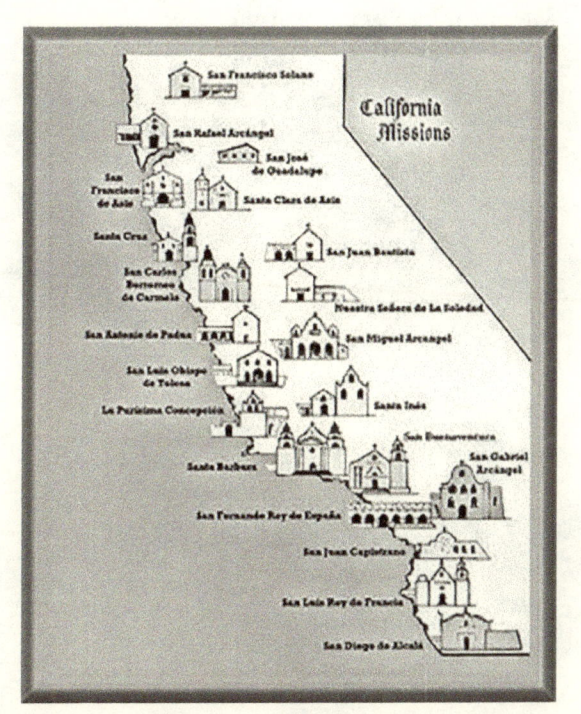

Missions Map - California Missions (missionscalifornia.com)

South to North
Mission Locations and Tribal Nations mentioned in book 3 are;

1. San Diego [Kumeyaay],
2. San Gabriel [Tongva],
3. Santa Barbara [Chumash],
4. Carmel/Monterey [Esselen],
5. San Juan Baptista [Mutsun],
6. San Jose [Muwekma],
7. San Francisco [Ohlone],
8. Sacramento [Nisenan/Patwin], &
9. Sutter's Mill [Miwok/Maidu]

# Broken Promises – Resource Guide

**For more information about the** persons and events featured in this historic fiction see the following resources:

1. *Who Would Have Thought It?* [1872] and *The Squatter and the Don* [1885] by Maria Amparo Ruiz Reprinted by Houghton Mifflin [2007] ISBN 978-0-618-48282-5
2. *The Treaty of Guadalupe Hidalgo: A Legacy of Conflict* by Richard Griswold del Castillo Ventura Public Library, Port Hueneme, CA 973.62 Bar code: R0011598113
3. *Governor Alvarado at the Santa Barbara Presidio Raises a Flag of California (Sovereign) Independence from Mexico in 1836* Noticias de Santa Barbara Historical Society, Vol. XV, No.4, Pg.23
4. *6 Generations : A Chumash Native American Narrates her Family Story* by Ernestine De Soto, Santa Barbara Museum of Natural History. Recorded at www.der.org [2011]
5. *Juan Alvarado: Governor of California 1836-1842* by Robert Ryal Miller University of Oklahoma Press [1998] ISBN 0-8061-3077-6

6. *Negotiating Conquest: Gender and Power in California 1770's to 1880's* by Miroslava Chavez-Garcia, University of Arizona Press [2004] ISBN 978-0-8165-2600-0
7. *Imperfect Union: How Jessie & John Fremont Mapped the West* by Steve Inskeep Penguin Press [2020]

CPSIA information can be obtained
at www.ICGtesting.com
Printed in the USA
LVHW022050170523
747248LV00004B/559

9 780967 330082